February 10th

I'm in London alone. Giancarlo was here for
two hours before his secretary telephoned
and said something important had come up –
something about a share certificate – and he
had to return immediately, via Rome.

Why am I melancholic? Doug and I discussed depression once. He told me that
health and characteristic mood may be governed by substances that flow through the
body, like phlegm, blood and bile, and this
belief predates the earliest Greek medical
texts. Melan-cholia is Greek for black bile.
He said that I am probably drowning in black
bile and then he laughed.

My melancholia is nothing to do with
black bile or blue mood, it's just the way I've
always been, my experience of life. Today we
flew first class, and Enrico picked us up and
carried our bags. It was all very luxurious,
but hardly real. I feel like a rotten egg in a
box, gift-wrapped with beautiful and expensive paper and the finest ribbon money can
buy.

Kate Morris was born in London in 1962. While
studying for a humanities degree she began writing
for *Tatler* magazine and the *Evening Standard*.
This book is her first novel and is not a compila-
tion of the column, *Single Girl's Diary*, that appeared in *Tatler*. She has also contributed to
Vanity Fair, the *Sunday Times* and *Vogue* and is
currently working on a novel and a film script.

KATE MORRIS

Single Girl's Diary

Mandarin

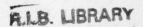

A Mandarin Paperback
SINGLE GIRL'S DIARY

First published in Great Britain 1996
by William Heinemann Ltd
This edition published 1997
by Mandarin Paperbacks
an imprint of Reed International Books Ltd
Michelin House, 81 Fulham Road, London SW3 6RB
and Auckland, Melbourne, Singapore and Toronto

A CIP catalogue record for this title
is available from the British Library
ISBN 0 7493 2106 7

Printed and bound in Great Britain
by BPC Paperbacks Ltd, Aylesbury, Bucks

To M.E.W. (1912–1975) with Love

Thank you to:

Maggie Phillips, Ed Victor and Louise Moore,

and to

Johanna Morris and Brian Alexander
Robert Fox and Fiona Golfar
Rafaella Barker and Hugh St Clair
Christopher Bowerbank

for letting me write this book at their houses

and to Geraldine Ogilvy for the use of her poem

and Peter Evans for his endless encouragement.

Keep a diary
and one day it will keep you

Mae West

March 25th

'He's dead.' Giles said. 'Sorry.'

The world wavered. 'What happened?' My voice was light and small. I flung myself on the battered sofa and began to sob. When I pulled myself up, exhausted and weak, the yellow, smiley-face clock was bomb-ticking loud in the pressured silence. Giles had dumped the limp, bloody, body on a piece of newspaper, and now he was smoking a cigarette.

'He was about to pounce on the chickens. He looked like a large rat.'

'Rats don't pounce,' I sobbed again.

'They do,' he said, 'Oh yes they do. Rats pounce on their prey.'

Giles entertains himself every evening by committing a few murders. He shoots rabbits, pigeons, crows, and dogs. Once he shot his own fetid foot. He'd taken an acid tab and in his hallucinatory state imagined his foot had a life of its own and was going to devour the rest of his body, limb by limb.

A *rat*. How could he have mistaken my beautiful, beloved cat for a rat. 'A rat,' I said, throwing my cup of tea at him, 'A rat. You knew it was my cat you lying BASTARD.'

So it really is the end. It has been the beginning of the end for about six months, but this episode is insurmountable. Maybe it needed to happen. It

1

gave me the strength to pack my bag for real. God I've packed my bag a dozen times, but this time, I packed with new strength – a rage-strength. Giles stood lazily in the bedroom doorway watching me. 'You'll be back,' he said at last. 'You won't be able to stay away. Where are you going anyway? Back to mad Mummy?'

'Fuck off Giles.'

Giles hated the cat. He used to kick him. And every time he saw him curled up in a small black and white ball on our bed he pushed him off. 'You'll be back,' he called after my taxi.

'Fuck off,' I shouted out of the window.

'Sorry,' I said to the driver, Tom Jones, who lives in the village, 'I won't be back. I'm off to London. Tom would it be all right, do you mind if I write a cheque?'

I dropped Tipsy in a box covered by a bloody white towel at Mr Wallace's vet surgery in town. He's going to be cremated.

I'm on the train. Raging rain slaps the window in diagonal streaks. The image of that hapless, blasted-up body is tormenting me and I'm wiping my tears with a British Rail napkin. There is a man sitting opposite me twirling the end of a pencil around in his ear, shaking it up and down, very fast, and then removing it and studying the tip. I would change seats but the train is full.

I'm going to my parents' house in World's End, which will be really weird. I've lived in Dorset for the last three years and although I've seen my cousin Sapphire, and my best friends, Beatrice, Tricky and

2

Matthew during that time I've really lost touch with London life. I left home six years ago when my mother told me she needed space. She said she had lost her identity and could no longer cope with just feeling like a wife and mother. That was when she asked me to call her Stella.

I always wished for a big, huggy mama, who would bake me sponge cakes with cream and jam filling and give me ice-cream made to look like a train with banana wheels and a chocolate funnel, like Mrs Hunt who lived next door made for her son, Jamie. I longed for Stella to tell me fairy stories while I listened, curled up in her lap, but she was slim and neurotic and cooked unfriendly vegetarian dishes made with lentils and spices that she always seemed to be testing for a potential cook book, that never quite got off the ground. She's not someone I can rely on. We tolerate each other. Agree not to disagree. And Dad is a flake.

I telephoned her from the station and said I was on my way home. My dream-Mama would have cooed and ahed and said darling how lovely to have you back, but Stella flapped and flipped and said she wouldn't be home before seven. If only magic Aunt May was here, I could go and stay with her for a while, but she's in Egypt.

March 26th

I can see Stella in the garden pruning roses. It's raining and she's wearing one of those horrible flower-patterned plastic shower caps. She's gesticulating in an odd way and talking to herself.

Madness obviously runs in families. It was crazy to move in with Giles. I remember the first time we drove to his house near Sherborne. Warning bells chimed but I ignored them. It was late and he had been drinking. He drove on to the wrong side of the dual carriageway in an abandoned and manic fashion but when I screamed he laughed.

I was attracted to the danger and the way he laughs. He laughs rarely, so that when he does you know it is for real. He laughs without opening his mouth. He's fearless and will always go one step further than most people which can be quite exciting. And he liked me. He doesn't really like women, but he liked me. He said I was more daring than other girls.

Stella was upset about the cat. She loves animals. She gives most of her love to her dog. She is a strict vegetarian, anti-bloodsports, exporting livestock and bull-fighting. She's not very sympathetic about my bust-up with Giles. 'Just as well,' she said, 'he's a loser, a ridiculous person.'

'He's not ridiculous,' I said, surprising myself with the vigour of my defence. 'You don't know him. He's just a bit confused.'

March 29th

I haven't telephoned anyone since arriving in London. I lie on the bed in the rosy spare room that used to be mine, and stare at the ceiling. I am obviously wasting my time but I don't really care. I am heartbroken about my dead cat and on the verge of hysteria. It is very unsettling, being alone, waking up without

4

Giles beside me. Even though he's a barbarian, I'm quite hurt that he has made no attempt to contact me.

Stella is sitting downstairs watching a programme about bees. Dad moved out again three weeks ago and is living in his office in Kensington. He's having yet another affair with a twenty-three-year-old *au pair* girl, whom he met on a train, which is too boring and inevitable to contemplate.

I've just been downstairs. Stella is crushing a small dark berry. She claims she is making tea but I suspect that she may be trying to kill herself. I once read that a man in middle America tried to poison his wife by planting mistletoe berries in a bowl of pasta. 'Stella?' I said. 'Are those mistletoe berries?'

'I've no idea,' she said, 'I bought them at the health food shop.'

'Maybe you should check,' I said.

'Why?' she asked.

'Oh, it's just that, I read . . .'

'What?'

'Nothing,' I said, suddenly feeling tired. 'Just be careful never to eat mistletoe berries.'

We sat there at the kitchen table. She sipping her weirdo tea humming and staring into the middle distance and me slugging a diet Coke and examining the ingrowing hairs on my legs. She popped a green and white pill. 'What's that?' I asked.

She showed me the box – Prozac.

April 1st

I'm in limbo land. Everyone else seems to have a life, playing April Fool's on each other, no doubt.

5

This morning I was feeling a bit desperate and rather hoped that Giles would turn up in his Citroën and take me away.

I finally made a telephone call. I telephoned my friend Matthew Clivesmith. 'Where are you?' he asked. 'What's happened? I telephoned you in Dorset and Giles said you had left.'

'Is that all he said?' I asked.

'Yes. Now what is going on?'

I told him the whole sick story. The shot cat, my Prozac-popping mother, my philandering father, and my pathetic state. He really perked up at the mention of Prozac. He says he knows a man on Prozac, a doctor who claims he is researching the effects before prescribing it to his patients.

'What happens to people on Prozac?' I asked. It evens them out, he told me, so that there are no highs or lows in their lives. It's a bland life, rather like eating food without salt.

Stella says she will never have Dad back, but of course she would if he came crawling.

April 4th

I received a postcard from Sapphire, posted here, because she had lost my Dorset address. The card was sent weeks ago, but she writes that she is returning in a couple of days. She says she visited the abandoned sixteenth-century capital of Fatehpur Sikri, where the emperor's sleeping quarters are called the Palace of Dreams. That would appeal to her, she likes to write her dreams down. She's been away for three months and I've really missed her.

Matthew sent me an article about Prozac. According to an American psychiatrist, taking Prozac is the 'mental equivalent of plastic surgery . . . Prozac transforms . . . the depressed, making them dramatically more confident and less fearful of rejection . . .'

I need some. Stella hasn't said that much about Dad leaving. Perhaps the effects of Prozac have mellowed the situation. He's left before, but never for this long. The last time was about five years ago. But Stella is that much older now and she's paranoid about ageing.

I spent hours on the telephone, first with Tricky and then with Beatrice. Tricky said she had never liked Giles, in fact, she said, she hated him. 'He's so aggressive,' she said. It really pissed me off, but I held back from telling her that he couldn't stand her either. He never saw the point of her and thought she was hard and cold. Beatrice wants a baby, which seems insane as she can hardly look after herself.

'Anna, get off the telephone,' Stella shouted. 'I need to call my doctor.' It was like the old days. Stella shouting up at me as I lay in the rose bedroom, writing sheets of morose poetry, feeling misunderstood and plotting my escape. I have to find somewhere to live. That is the next most important thing to do.

April 6th

Sapphire telephoned from the airport this morning and then came straight here. She looks brown, thin and wistful. We sat in the kitchen for five hours, smoking and drinking cups of tea and eating toast with Marmite. Stella kept popping in and out and trying to get her to eat. 'A little lasagne? A Scandinavian salad? Some tiny tomatoes?'

'No I'm fine with toast, thank you,' she repeated over and over again.

Stella adores Sapphire. She worshipped Sapphire's mother, Izzy, her sister who was only eleven months older. Aunt Izzy died four years ago after a fatal mixture of sleeping pills and drink. She was devastated because her husband, Sapphire's father, Jack, had left her for a young boy whom he had met in San Francisco. Aunt May is about twenty years older than Stella. She was the most beautiful and vibrant of the three sisters, known far and wide for her wit and charm. Stella always says that May wasn't that interested in her two younger siblings. She is still quite in awe of May and always on best behaviour when they are together. In fact she is quite jealous, I think, that I get on so well with May.

When Stella went out to walk her yappy dog Pixie, we talked about Dad and his hopeless drunken affairs. He used to be a regular drinker, the odd glass of whisky before dinner, but Sapphire thinks he's now drinking nearly all the time. She had lunch with him just before she left for India and apparently he drank two Bloody Marys and one and a half bottles of wine.

Sapphire and I both agreed we feel lonely. We sat in silence after admitting this, and then we began to giggle. I asked her to stay the night. She's sharing my bed. She's here now asleep.

8

April 8th

We lay around yesterday feeling more and more neurotic. We had been invited to a party given by a couple of friends of Sapphire's. Artdealers, Christian Trent and Hock Dickenson.

We dressed, re-dressed, decided we couldn't go, and then, at the last minute, we found some Valium next to Stella's bed and took a couple each. We managed to get to the Cobden Club in a mini-cab, and were greeted by a man holding a tray of cranberry juice and vodka cocktails – delicious. After a couple of drinks the pills began to kick in and I felt very loose and floppy.

We were pretty spaced out. I vaguely remember a crush of people saying, 'How are you?' and kissing me 'mmmwa, mmmwa' on both cheeks. I said, 'I feel depressed,' to a dwarf-like dead boring man whom I've known for years and he fled. At one point some flamenco music came on and a man charged at me with his hands pointed up by his ears. I presume he was miming a bull. He introduced himself as Greg something, an American – and he said, 'You look as though you could do with a drink, you seem depressed.' I think he'd overheard my line to the dwarf.

Anyway, when the party wound down at about three, Sapphire and I shared a cab with Greg to his house in Colville Mews, for a post-party party. About twenty people arrived, but I don't remember anything past that point. I've just spoken to Sapphire on the telephone, hoping she would fill in the gaps. She said an Italian man dropped us home, in his chauffeur-driven car, and apparently I gave him my telephone number, address and a lingering goodnight kiss.

April 11th

I had a drink with the American, Greg. He telephoned three times yesterday from his mobile. Once he called when he was playing tennis which is a particularly strange thing to do. Perhaps it was the moment they were changing ends. He then called half an hour later and we had rather an intimate conversation. He asked me what I was wearing which was a touch cheeky and then he said, 'What are you up to for the next few days? Let's hook up.'

'I'm desperate for a job, and I need to find somewhere to have lunch.'

'Lunch? I'm sure we could arrange that. Tomorrow?'

'Oh God, I mean live.' We laughed a while, me more hysterically than him. 'I need to find somewhere to live.'

'Move in with me. I have a spare room. What kind of job?'

'A famous filmstar,' I said. 'No joking, I would like to act. I've always wanted to act.'

'We will discuss it all,' he said, 'tonight. Groucho seven o'clock.'

He's a funny little thing. Not like those huge, hulking Americans brought up on milk and steak. He's small and dark, smart, brash and crude, perfect for his job. (He has his own PR company and acts as personal agent to some of his clients.) Not that I would trust him. He's obviously rather fickle.

His head darted here and there checking to see who was leaving and who was coming in. He waved at Stephen Fry who waved back in a bemused fashion. During coffee he said, 'Get out there, girl. If you want to act, you have to make the contacts. I know this guy, Henry Irving, a big producer. He's staying in London for a week or two. You should meet him. Perhaps I'll get him over. I need to talk to him.'

'That would be great,' I said, smiling in what I thought was a flirtatious and appealing manner. 'You really are very kind. Thank you, darling.'

April 16th

It's heaven to be away from that mad, depressed, house in the World's End. I'm travelling to Rome with a man I hardly know. Giancarlo di Trevi, the man who dropped Sapphire and me off the other night after Greg's post-party party. It all happened so fast. A large bouquet of white lilies arrived last week, with a note saying 'Love Giancarlo', and a telephone number. Of course I telephoned a couple of days later, to say thank you, and he asked me to have lunch with him, the next day. I said I'd love to. We arranged to meet at Le Caprice. I was about to say, 'How will I know you?' when he offered to send his driver to pick me up.

The driver, Enrico, was very punctual. I was feeling rather despondent that day, because Greg had telephoned moments before to cancel the afternoon meeting he'd set up with the 'big' producer, Henry

Irving. He told me that Mr Irving had to return to LA to deal with some urgent business and would be back in about a week.

Enrico asked me if I had any bags and I said, 'Under my eyes, yes, but no, I'm only going to lunch.'

'Oh my sorry,' he said. 'Yes you are the young lady who will have lunch with the Count di Trevi.'

'The count?'

'Mr Giancarlo.'

'Yes, that's me, I mean that's not me, but I'm the one meeting him for lunch, at Le Caprice.'

How many other girls were being driven around London, dropped off or picked up at airports? Suddenly I felt a fool. Finally I said, 'Excuse me I only met Mr di Trevi for a moment. I can hardly remember what he looks like.' Enrico laughed and offered me a cigarette.

'The count,' he laughed again, 'not so tall, not so small.'

'Is that it?'

'Not fat, not thin . . . .'

'Does he have many girlfriends? Is he married?'

'No wife,' he laughed. 'But sometimes there are ladies, not for long, because he never stays long. He's a busy man.'

'Does he send flowers to these ladies?'

'Now that is a question I cannot answer. Why? He sent flowers to you?'

I smiled and nodded.

I arrived at the Caprice first. A waiter asked me if I wanted a newspaper to look at. 'Yes please,' I said gratefully. I hid behind a story about a woman who is suing a dating agency because the man she was sent to meet was: 'Ugly spotty and obese with halitosis . . .'

Giancarlo put my hand to his lips when he came to the table and apologised for being ten minutes late. He was taller than I had expected, good looking, clean and neat, and his cuff-links had a crest on them. He smelt of crushed lime. He was wearing a suit and an expensive tie, so unlike Giles in every way. Every way. He let me talk and I think I needed to. I told him all about the last few weeks. He was so easy, he laughed, and the more he laughed the more I exaggerated the story, until Giles had killed the cat with an automatic machine gun and a hand grenade, blowing up his foot in the process.

'This man, Giles,' he said, at last, 'what kind of man is this, who could shoot your kitten?'

'My cat, yes, I don't know, perhaps his father sexually abused him when he was a child.' Tears were welling when he passed me a smooth, stiff, linen handkerchief and took my hand.

'Sorry, I don't mean to make you unhappy. I would like to see you very happy.'

When he looked at me with such concern I believed that this was the man who would save me, save me from Stella and Dad, and Giles and poverty and the last three years. That is why when he asked me to Italy for a long weekend I accepted without hesitation, because I know he is too polite to force himself on me, though of course all the girls said he would be expecting to. I'm not so sure, he's too sophisticated. When I see him sitting next to me reading his papers so intently, I feel like lying on his lap and disturbing him in some way.

April 17th

We are in Rome, staying in his family's flat in the via Vittoria near the Spanish steps. God, everything is so beautiful, so vibrant, so *dolce*. The sun, the people, the food. I would go so far as to say this is the most beautiful city I have ever seen, not that I have seen that much of it yet. Giancarlo has put me in the spare room, with its own bathroom and terrace. Over the terracotta rooftops floats the sound of cellos, pianos and flutes from a music school at the end of the street. We had dinner last night in a small divine restaurant, where I ate a mound of spinach topped with chopped liver, delicious.

As far as I can make out, Giancarlo invests in business projects, and then is paid back with interest. He is based in New York, although he has a flat in London, and his parents own this flat and another in Paris.

After dinner he took me for ice-cream in the Piazza Navona. A small dirty gypsy child tried to sell us a rose, but Giancarlo shooed her away like a dog, which upset me. I told him that Rome was the most beautiful city I have ever seen and how I would love to live here. 'You would not like to live here,' he said. 'Nothing happens in Rome. Nothing gets done. Rome is a dead city.' That really depressed me. How could anyone feel dead living somewhere like this?

I wondered whether he would come into my room, not that I wanted him to. We had eaten very late, and he said he was very tired. I was too, and planned to feign sound sleep if he did come in. But he didn't, and in the end it was better that way, because although he is kind and sweet and his way of life attracts me, I can't imagine a passionate encounter with him. Giles and I never went anywhere of course, his idea of going away meant taking a whole load of drugs and a tent to a music festival. We never had any money, so getting in meant climbing over fences and dodging dogs.

April 19th

We are staying with his parents in a castle overlooking a village in Umbria. His mother, Domitilla speaks very good English, but when she lapses into Italian with Giancarlo, I can only understand a third of what they are saying. Domitilla is so chic that no matter what I put on I always feel clumpy and foolish. My black and white checked trousers that looked so smart in London are now creased and there is a red wine spot on the thigh. My linen dress has several small holes in it and my shoes with the buckles are scuffed.

His father doesn't speak much, and when he does he mumbles so incoherently that it is impossible to understand what he is saying. It's just as well that he spends most of the time in his studio painting still lives of melons and figs.

After dinner last night GC and I walked in the olive groves. We then went back and sat on the terrace and talked for a long time. He said I remind him of a wounded wild animal, rescued from a trap. That touched me. 'You are very beautiful,' he said,

15

'but you don't know that you are. You hide behind all that hair, all those ripped clothes.'

'And you are far too smart,' I said. I had drunk a few glasses of red wine and I loosened his tie, and undid a couple of buttons on his shirt. He smiled at me, that indulgent, I'm falling in love with your smile. 'You should relax a bit more,' I said, pouring him another drink. I leant over and took off his glasses. He kissed me on the lips, and the wine and the warm air made me kiss him back more passionately than I had intended.

'*Bellissima* baby,' he said after the kiss. 'You don't know this, but one day you will be mine.'

'No,' I said, 'I don't belong to anyone. I have just freed myself from three years of living someone else's life. I want to be my own person. I don't know what is happening to me at the moment. I don't even have a permanent place to live.'

'Listen, Anna, I have been thinking. For the time being, my flat in London is empty. Why don't you stay there?'

It's all too easy, he's rescuing me, and it's wonderful, but there is a nagging instinct telling me something is wrong. But of course it is too tempting an offer to turn down. 'Giancarlo,' I said, 'are you sure? God, darling, that would be sublime.'

April 24th

My life is accelerating and changing at such an unnerving pace. Giancarlo went straight back to New York and Enrico met me at Heathrow, with a set of keys. I've moved my few possessions from

Stella's into Giancarlo's huge flat in Holland Park Gardens. He rents the first floor, which has a large, high-ceilinged drawing room and tall windows that look out over the communal gardens.

This luxury cannot compare to Giles and his squalid freezing cottage from Hell, full of never-ending washing-up and dirty stinking socks. Giancarlo's flat is so graceful with its high ceilings, and fireplaces inlaid with intricate mosaics. The study has a huge television and a cupboard full of indexed videos and four Matisse drawings on the wall. There is a portrait by Ingres in his bedroom and a Degas pastel, a ballerina tying her shoe, in the dining room.

There is a Spanish girl who lives here called Maria. She is meant to be Giancarlo's house-keeper, but she looks more like a sultry art student. She has large green eyes, lightly tanned long limbs, a dirty laugh and she walks around barefoot. I think she thinks that I am Giancarlo's mistress being set up in his London pad and although that couldn't be further from the truth, the whole situation makes me feel a touch uncomfortable.

This afternoon, Maria asked me if I wanted some tea. 'I'd love some,' I said, a little too earnestly. Half an hour later I was still waiting. I walked into the kitchen to see what was happening. She was sitting listening to some kind of French rap and painting her nails.

'Is the tea ready?' I asked a touch timidly.

'Oh.' She sat up. 'I am so sorry. I forgot.' It was all one big wind-up, some kind of power trip.

I spoke to Giancarlo about Maria just now on the

telephone. He said that she's been living in the flat for nearly a year.

'Do you think she's annoyed I've moved in?' I asked.

'It is not her business to be annoyed,' he said. 'She is paid well to look after the flat and keep it clean. It is my decision to have a friend living there, nothing to do with her.'

'But, Giancarlo, she hates me. I think she must be in love with you.'

'*Non è vero*,' he said. 'How can she be? I have been in the flat perhaps six weeks in the year.'

'So?' I said. 'One month, one day, it doesn't matter. It may have been an instantaneous reaction, a *coup de foudre*.'

'Please calm down,' he said. 'I will talk with her.'

'No don't,' I said, fearful that she may turn into a vengeful Mrs Danvers character, the housekeeper from Hell.

'By the way,' he said, 'perhaps that is what happened when I first saw you at that party in your long black velvet coat, with the pale white face under all the long dark hair. Those dreamy eyes . . .'

'What happened?' I asked, knowing what he meant.

'This *coup de foudre*,' he said. I giggled, but now I know that he does not just want to be my friend, and although I knew that already I didn't want it confirmed.

April 26th

Greg The Mobile took me out last night to a party, for the opening of a new restaurant that he PRs for. I agreed to go with him because he promised me that Henry The Big Producer would be there. On the way, between a couple of mobile telephone calls to the restaurant, he told me that he had invited some A-list celebrities to the opening, people like Tarrantino, and Madonna, who happen to be in London, but in fact he was fearful that a whole load of weather girls would turn up, definitely C-list. Willem Dafoe was at the party, but no sign of the Henry 'the Big' Irving. I asked Greg whether Dafoe was A- or B-list celebrity. He thinks more B.

'Come back with me, for one last drink,' Greg said at the end of a very long night.

'No, I'm very tired,' I said.

'I'll wake you up,' he said. 'Try me.'

'Please just take me home, I'm exhausted,' I pleaded. When he dropped me off at last, I felt I had to ask him if he'd like a cup of coffee.

'Do you have anything else?' he asked.

'Diet Ribena?' Another pause. 'Or a boiled egg?'

He looked absolutely disgusted and said, 'Yuk, that's the ultimate turn-off.'

'Oh God,' I said, the tears streaming down my face with laughter, 'I'm sorry, Greg, but it's goodnight for me, goodnight darling.'

This morning Maria announced that she was going on holiday tomorrow for two weeks. I asked her whether Giancarlo knew and she said that it had all been arranged weeks ago. Her sister is getting

19

married, in Spain.

'Don't forget to feed the feesh,' she said. 'The Count di Trevi loves, no worships, these feesh.'

April 27th

Greg telephoned this morning and said that Henry was definitely on for a drink tonight at Blakes, where he's staying. 'Are you sure he'll be there?' I asked.

'One hundred per cent,' Greg said, 'for sure.'

When I arrived ten minutes late, Greg said that Henry had left a message that he'd been called away at the last moment for a big meeting with a big lawyer. 'What can I say?' Greg said. 'Jesus the man is harder to get to than Clinton.' Frankly it really was the end, because it meant I was stuck with Greg alone again. As a last ditch attempt to make something out of a nothing evening I asked him if there was any work I could do at his agency. He said he would think of something.

April 28th

Greg The Mobile telephoned at nine this morning and suggested I have lunch with a man he knows, a features editor who works for a Sunday magazine. He said he was meant to be having lunch with him at Kensington Place, but couldn't make it and perhaps it would be a good idea if I took his place, because this man might be able to give me some work.

'But I'm not a journalist,' I said.

'No problem,' Greg said.

'Does he have any idea that I'm coming?'

'Not yet,' Greg said, 'but I'll let him know.'

Lunch went on for far too long. The man, Edward, big and bulky, stained shirt and bulge under his chin, was waiting for me at the table, with a glass of champagne. 'Have one too,' he said. 'Expenses.' He spent the first half an hour slagging off Greg. He said that Greg had literally been driven out of New York. 'This town ain't big enough for the two of us' kind of thing, because he had such an appalling reputation in business and with women. 'It got to the point,' Edward said, 'where he literally couldn't show his face anywhere. He was clinging desperately to a raft. A dead man who just happened to be alive.'

'So if you despise him so much why have lunch with him?' I asked.

'He's good for stories,' Edward said. 'Always has a few celeb-style stories. He's a devil when it comes to dishing the dirt.'

Edward raved on about the riotous time he'd had in the seventies, and then he told me he had been working on a novel for thirteen years. He ordered a bottle of wine for himself and the plot unfolded, paragraph by paragraph. It seemed to concern a few homosexual encounters and some class A drugs. It was dead boring and I decided that I must get some work out of him to make up for sitting through it all. 'Sounds very interesting,' I said. 'Have you found a publisher?'

'No,' he said.

'I'm sure you will though.'

'No I don't think so. Things are not going so well for me at the moment. Yesterday I was banned from driving for a year.'

21

'Oh God, poor you. How awful. Do you think ... Could I, can I borrow your car?' I laughed, never expecting anything to come of it.

'I don't see why not,' he said to my amazement, flinging some keys across the table.

'Wow. Thanks, darling. Are you sure? That is so kind of you.'

He then told me that he wanted to commission a piece about weekend drug takers. 'Remember that children's TV programme Crackerjack on a Friday afternoon? It's Friday, it's five o'clock, it must be Crackerjack. Well, the opening line of this article could be. It's Friday, it's 5 o'clock, it must be crack 'n' smack. Would you be interested?'

'Not really,' I said. 'But I'd love to do anything else.' In the end he commissioned me to do some research for a piece called Bouncing Black. 'You know,' he said, 'black clothes are back.'

'But black never goes out of fashion,' I said.

'Yeh,' he said. 'But it's a catchy title.' My job is to find out which celebs wear black and what is their favourite black item of clothing. Dead boring, but it's an easy £400 because all I'll have to do is talk to Greg.

April 30th

Yesterday I finally met Henry The Big Producer for a big breakfast at Blakes. He's certainly an enormous eater. He shook my hand long and hard and looked me deep in the eye. 'So,' he said, stuffing nearly a whole piece of toast into his mouth, looking me up and down and down and up, until I was cringing in

22

my seat and wishing I could be swallowed up. 'So,' he said, again, louder this time, 'my friend Greg says you may be perfect for a part in the school movie.'

Greg had given me a ten-minute brief that morning. 'What a brilliant idea,' I said, 'I just love it. A new St Trinian's-style movie. It would be perfect for me. You see, I have real life experience, I went to a British boarding school for a while.'

'Did you?' he said. 'Well that helps and you look the part and love that accent.' He was already looking at his big Breitling watch. 'Have to fly,' he said. 'Why don't we give you a go? It will be a small part.'

'That's fine,' I said, wanting the meeting to end before he changed his mind.

'Well we'll be in touch,' he said, standing up and shaking my hand long and hard again.

'I look forward to hearing from you,' I said, literally skipping in a St Trinian-style fashion out of the hotel and practically hopping to where I had parked Edward's car. It's a battered, cream-coloured old Mercedes and the windscreen is literally covered in birdshit. There are whisky bottles on the floor and a hundred cigarette butts in the ashtray, but it works and it has a Kensington and Chelsea permit.

Giancarlo telephoned just now to say he is arriving the night after tomorrow for two days. The flat is in a state of disarray. I did a quick panic hoover, tomorrow I will start on the washing-up. Anything is possible now that I have a part in a movie, albeit a small one.

May 1st

I woke up this morning to find that all Giancarlo's tropical fish were floating dead at the top of the tank. I had unplugged the heating system when I did my panic hoover last night. There was no time to freak. I telephoned Matthew and he suggested finding replicas. I scooped all the dead fish out and put them in a plastic bag. I then drove around like a maniac going to weird pet shops all over town trying to match the dead fish with new ones. I got four out of five. As a last resort I went to Harrods' pet department where I found a fifth, black and yellow, fish, which is not an exact replica, but it will do but when I rushed back to the car it was gone. Edward's bird-shit-covered Mercedes had been towed away because I had parked in a meter bay instead of a residents'.

I took a taxi back to Giancarlo's and then decided to leave the car in the pound, because I don't have the money to take it out. I poured the new fish into the tank and then packed a few things and came to Stella's. It seems easier to be here while Giancarlo is in town.

'So you're back,' she said. 'What happened to the boyfriend?'

'He's not my boyfriend, and nothing has happened,' I said.

Aunt May has returned from Egypt. I had a long conversation with her on the telephone and told her I had met a producer and he had offered me a part in a big Hollywood movie. She was very impressed, and delighted that I have left Giles. 'Such a depressing character,' she said, 'so sullen and diffident.'

24

May 3rd

Giancarlo telephoned last night from the flat. 'Where are you?' he asked. 'You don't have to leave because I'm here.'

'I thought it was better,' I said, 'to give you some privacy.'

'There are three bedrooms.'

'I know, but . . .'

'I had forgotten that Maria is away. I will feed the fish tonight. Are they all right? Jaws looks paler.'

'Um, they seem fine,' I said, 'swimming well.'

'Good,' he said. 'Well why don't we have dinner tomorrow?'

'Love to,' I said, 'that would be lovely.'

May 10th

Edward has been leaving messages about the Bouncing Black piece, due in tomorrow. I have managed to find a few names, more C- or D-list than A, but I am having a last fling with Greg about it tomorrow morning. Edward enquired about the car and I was crushed with shame. It's been in the pound for ten days, and there is a daily storage fee, so the amount will be so excessive by now that it will hardly be worth retrieving it.

Giancarlo and I had dinner last week. It was fine, because Tricky and Beatrice came as well and diluted any potential passion. He telephones me every morning at eight o'clock his time, one o'clock here. I am rarely in but when I return there are usually two or even three messages on the machine. He telephones again in the early evening and occasionally he calls very late. There have been moments when I can't think what to say, particularly if I have already spoken to him once, so I find myself expressing banal thoughts – 'God, I must do some more exercise,' or 'Maybe I should cut my hair but on the other hand maybe I should grow it out.'

Maria is back from holiday, tanned and skulking around in a tiny white dress. She showed me some photographs of her sister's wedding – a troop of tiny children dressed up in flamenco dresses, a long table

26

laden with festive drink and food, pastel confetti, purple and yellow flowers, a white and pink bouquet flying through the air. Her mother must have had an affair with an American marine because her sister mother and father are dark and small but Maria is blonde and quite tall.

May 11th

Spent the morning at Greg's office, typing the last draft of 'Black is Back' and then faxing it off. Greg wanted to use his own clients of course, so he cannily rolled off a few fictitious facts. He said that Sting's favourite piece of black clothing is a waistcoat that he wore for his first live gig, Clive Anderson's a bow-tie that he borrowed for a graduation dinner and never returned, Marco Pierre White's a black T-shirt, given to him by a girl he had a passionate crush on at the age of sixteen, and Amanda de Cadenet's a black wonder bra.

He hasn't heard anything from Henry The Big Producer since the morning after the drink at Blakes when they spoke briefly on the telephone. Henry apparently promised that he would use me in the film, but nothing has yet been confirmed. I tried to persuade Greg to call him, but he said it was better to wait a while.

When I got home there was a message from Edward thanking me for the fax, but he says he needs a couple more hip and cooler celebs. That threw me and I was beginning to wonder whether all the rushing around was worth a measly £400. I was racking my brains about who to telephone next

27

when the depraved Giles turned up at the door. He's here now. He looks terrible and says he is depressed. He claims he can't live without me, so why isn't he dead? He has a manic lost look in his eye. I don't know what to do, who to telephone. 'Got yourself a posh pad,' he said. 'What happened? Poor little girl ran away from her murderous boyfriend and found herself a sugar-daddy?'

That hit a nerve and I told him that it was all over between us, but his wild rebellious aura still holds a certain allure. He appeals to my darker side and in a sick way I am quite pleased that he has made the effort to track me down. He went to Stella's house first and she gave him my address. I left a message on her machine: 'Thanks Stella for sending the Devil round here.'

Maria is in the kitchen with Giles. She's chosen this particular moment to clean the floor in her tiny white dress. Pert little bottom stuck in the air, the lacy knickers alarmingly white against her honey-thighs. Giles is agog – of course. I want to get him out, but I'm scared that he may do something foolish like shoot me or squeeze washing-up liquid into the fish tank.

An hour has passed since I left Giles in the kitchen and locked myself in the bedroom. I've just been back there, ostensibly to make a cup of tea, but really to see what was going on. There was an empty bottle of champagne on the table and two glasses. 'Hope you don't mind,' Giles said, nodding at the bottle. I didn't reply, but Maria who looked a little ruffled and flushed sniggered and when I left the room they laughed.

28

He's just been in. He lay down next to me, then he turned on his side and put his arm around me and said he was truly sorry about the cat. 'It was a horrible mistake. I love you baby,' he said, 'my own kitten.' He was unshaven and smelt of sweat, but he looked so tortured and pained that it was quite pathetic, almost touching. He had a cigarette burning in his right hand and I asked him to go and flush it down the loo. He pulled his left arm from me and rolled across the bed, accidentally tipping the ash on the white bedspread and making a small hole. I told him he was a slut and he called me a bourgeois bitch and we had a huge fight. I asked him to leave but he said he had nowhere else to stay. It's hopeless. I'm going to telephone Giancarlo.

May 12th

Giancarlo arrived this morning from New York to rescue me! Giles was crashed out on the sofa. He hadn't even taken off his mud-encrusted boots. Giancarlo shook him awake and asked him to leave. Giles was taken aback by Giancarlo's dominant manner and so was I. There was a moment of astounded silence before Giles said, 'Look mate, Anna's my girlfriend and I'm staying the night with her, all right?'

'No, it is not all right,' Giancarlo said. 'Anna is my guest and she does not appear to want you here.'

'You're not my boyfriend, Giles,' I added.

'So there is nothing much more to say,' Giancarlo said, ushering Giles to the door.

'Take your arm away,' Giles said, shaking him off and slamming the door.

Giancarlo stayed for lunch and then took the afternoon Concorde flight back to New York. It is the closest I have ever been to having a knight in shining armour save me from a potentially life-threatening situation.

Beatrice told me that Damien Hirst, master of hip and cool concept art, wears a back velvet Gianfranco Ferre jacket with thin white stripes when he is posing as a young artist around town. I faxed it in and Edward was delighted.

May 14th

Greg telephoned this morning and said that Henry The Big Producer had sent a fax. Shooting is scheduled to start in the second week of July and I will be needed for about three weeks. 'But what is my part?' I asked Greg.

'Don't worry about it, just get out there, that's the most important thing.' I haven't even seen a script but Greg says I shouldn't worry, because it will almost definitely be quite a small part and I won't have many words to learn.

'You'll be earning us big bucks babe,' he said.

That threw me. 'Us?'

'Yeh. I'm the agent, you're the client. I take twenty per cent.'

'Do you?'

'Yeh. Get a grip. I'm the agent, you're the actress. Guess who found you the part?'

I had no idea that Greg was my agent, we never discussed it. I thought he was being helpful, because he liked me or fancied me a little. It's true about him finding me a part, but his behaviour is a tad disingenuous.

I've found an acting school in Ealing which offers short acting courses. Two weeks cost about £300 so it means the car is going to have to linger in the pound. I feel I need to do a course before arriving on the set, because my only experience so far is acting at school, and embellishing anecdotes.

Stella telephoned this evening. She said that Dad has been in touch and she had given him my number. She sounded hollow, and is obviously very cut up by his defection. I'm worried about her and I suggested she finds a lodger so she's not so lonely.

May 18th

Dad invited me to lunch at La Familigia. I checked to make sure it would just be the two of us, because Stella would consider it an act of great treason if I ate in the presence of the *au pair*. We met today, for the first time since Christmas. He sat down, ordered himself a double whisky no ice, lit a cigarette and then announced that he wanted to divorce Stella.

'But Dad,' I said. 'Why? Why now? Can't you see what a cliché you are. A middle-aged man who drinks too much, abandons his wife for a Swedish *au pair* girl.'

'She's a New Zealander.'

'Whatever, Dad, it's irrelevant. Why do it? If you must do it, why do you have to desert Stella. Why can't you have an affair in *cinq à sept* fashion like the French? By the way, did you know she's on Prozac?'

'Yes.' Dad looked glum. 'I've spoken to her. She's like a marshmallow. Why doesn't she do anything?'

'She's depressed. She hasn't been able to get down to her cookery writing, maybe she's going through the menopause, who knows? Why don't you give her a chance?'

'We don't even sleep in the same room,' he said.

'Yes, well. Look don't mention divorce just yet. Wait until she's found a lodger. She'll be in a better way by then.'

'A lodger?' he said. 'A male lodger?'

'Yes,' I said, knowing he was wound up. 'I think so.'

'But,' he said, slamming his drink down on the table, 'she can't have strange men living in the house.'

'Well Dad,' I said, 'whatyagoingtodoaboutit?!'

May 21st

Edward telephoned. The Bouncing Black piece is coming out tomorrow and then I will be paid. He asked how I was getting on with the car and I said fine. I'm terrified. I want to change my telephone number so that I never have to speak to him again. Then I'll send him a note saying I've moved abroad and give him the address of the car pound.

I just had a long conversation with Giancarlo and confessed about the car. He gave me the details of his Visa card and told me to go and deal with it. 'Oh Giancarlo,' I said, 'I don't think . . .'

'Do it,' he said to my relief, 'as quickly as possible.'

'I'll pay you back,' I said. 'Miss you.' God what would I do without him?

Perhaps I would marry the man I met last night at

32

Matthew's dinner party. He's called Douglas and he is so beautiful, so devastatingly handsome that it is quite daunting to contemplate. He has the eyes of a cat, the cheekbones of a tiger and a cruel, sensuous mouth. His hair is soft, thick and tawny-coloured and his eyes bluebell-blue. He's a script-writer with a seductive, twisted and unique view of life. When he laughs, which he does often, he is boyish and endearing and when he sneers, he does it in such a strange, comical way that I laugh compliantly, wanting to be on his side.

Wouldn't it be so much more interesting he said, if we were all sitting here in the nude. I laughed and then he said something like, well it would be better than all this slithering chit-chat. I told him about my imminent audition for the acting school and how I haven't yet found an audition piece and he offered to write one for me. I'm agonising about whether he will hunt my telephone number down.

May 22nd

I had lunch with Sapphire at 192 and we bought the newspaper and looked at the magazine and I was amazed to find BOUNCING BLACK spread across the middle page and underneath my name spelt out in bold letters. There were all the quotes, mostly made up by Greg, and a photograph of Sting wearing a black jacket and Amanda de Cadenet in a black corset.

We could only afford one course, so I went straight to the pudding, a gooseberry fool with shortbread on the side. Delicious. I told her about meeting Doug and then about Giancarlo's offer of paying to get the car.

33

She said I have to draw a line. 'But it would be a loan,' I said.

She smiled and raised her eyebrows and I laughed.

'It would be,' I protested feebly.

'Look whatever way you look at it, he would have even more hold over you than he does now. He's investing for a long-term future. It's unfair to let him do things like that when you are unsure of how you feel.'

'I know,' I sighed. Of course she's right, annoyingly so.

Anyway I've just spoken to him on the telephone and told him I won't be needing his credit card, so now I feel virtuous. I'll just have to telephone Edward again and ask if there is anything else I could do, after all £400 is better than a kick up the backside.

May 23rd

I telephoned Edward first thing and asked him if there was something I could do. I need the money, I was about to say, so that I can get your car out of the pound. 'Nothing I can think of right now,' he said brusquely.

'What about the weekend drug-takers?'

'No. It was done in one of the glossies this month.' Then there was a pause and he said, 'Look I may have something, meet me later. Come to the reception and we'll go for a drink.'

Edward took me to a basement wine bar and asked me to do a piece about what it would be like to suddenly have huge breasts.

'Keeping abreast of the new voluptuousness,' he said, smirking at his own ingenuity.

'Is that the new thing?' I asked naïvely.

'If we say so,' he said. It could be very funny he said. We want to know how you feel, do people react differently to you? Call my secretary, she has the name of a shop in Euston where they will fix you up with silicon breasts, the ones that transvestites wear.

I agreed so that I can pay for his car to be released.

I gave in tonight. I telephoned Matthew to ask how I could get hold of Doug. 'You too,' he said. 'I completely forgot to tell you he telephoned two or three days ago and asked for your number.'

May 25th

Doug telephoned this morning, while I was in the bath. When I heard the message, my heart was dancing and racing around, but I managed to wait a couple of cool, agonising, hours before returning the call. He's written a short script and he's coming over this evening to deliver it.

I went to the boob shop today. I walked past it several times because it was called TV Heaven, so I presumed it was a television repair shop or something. The shop assistants were kindly-looking middle-aged women with big peroxide hair. There were giant-sized bras and pink and black nylon knickers displayed on shop dummies and thick catalogues that one could flick through, to choose the naughtier gadgets.

I was kitted out with a 42DD cup-size pair of

boobs that feel like heavy, clammy, jelly. They had to be wedged into an enormous bra. The skin colour isn't quite right, and the top of the jelly sticks out of the top of the bra so I won't be able to wear anything too *décolleté*. I thought I might wear them when Doug comes round tonight. I want to see if he notices.

May 26th

Darling Doug. I borrowed one of Maria's tiny little tops and stuffed my huge appendages into it, and then put on a small fluffy cardigan. I was laughing and laughing when he came to the door and he looked a little startled. He sat down and I wanted to kiss him. He is so attractive, so good-looking. He didn't seem to notice my boobs, although they are such an encumbrance, I couldn't think of anything else. I'm sure some women enjoy their huge breasts, but I wouldn't. The lascivious glances from lusty men would mortify me.

He showed me the script. It's a little melodramatic but because Doug is the writer it doesn't seem to matter. It's a piece about a girl on the telephone, to her ex-boyfriend late at night. It starts off with her being perky, and then she spirals, becoming jealous, and acting like a victim. By the end she's threatening to kill herself. We went through it once or twice and then I got up and took off my cardigan. He still didn't say anything so I jumped up and down until at last he said, 'Are those real?'

'No,' I laughed.

'Good,' he said, 'now why don't you come here and I'll help you take them off.'

36

We went to buy a bottle of champagne in the off licence. Even walking down the street with him was an exciting, memorable event. It was like walking in a dream because everyone else looked so grey and depressed.

He stayed the night. He was no stranger. Kissing him was so sexy that I wanted to devour him. This morning I feel giddy and energised, impervious to any problems. My stomach rolls when I think about kissing him and about his hands which are so masculine and tanned.

May 27th

Maria was in tears today. I asked her what was the matter but she sobbed some more and put her head in her arms. I wanted to touch her and give some sign that I was sympathetic, so I said, 'Don't worry, Maria. If you want to talk about it, let me know.'

She sat up. 'Thank you,' she said. I stood a little awkwardly and then I squeezed her shoulders.

Doug is coming over late tonight. He telephoned today and called me sweetie.

May 28th

Found Maria sobbing again. 'What is it?' I asked softly.

'Anna,' she said. 'Oh my God. I'm pregnant.'

'Oh God, Maria. Do you want the baby?'

I knew immediately. I had a vision of Maria in the kitchen: alluring ass, short white dress, bare tanned thighs. Giles' legs sprawled out in a V, languid drag of a cigarette, a wanton half-smile, watching her as he would a porn video, misogynystic, growing harder. Pouring champagne, stroking her hair, kissing her neck, pulling her hand to his stiff crotch. Entering from behind, her hand slips on the wet cloth. It's all over in one quick moment and he's pulling up his zip, lighting another cigarette, walking out of the door and searching for me. That's the moment when he came and lay next to me on the bed with the half-smoked cigarette.

'I cannot have the baby,' she said. 'I not know the man at all.'

'Was it . . . ?'

'A man, your . . . I never knew his name.'

'I understand it was a man, but was it . . . that day in the kitchen . . . Giles . . . ?'

'No,' she said, sobbing violently now. 'Forgive me. Yes with him, with Geeles.'

May 30th

I took Maria to a pregnancy advisory bureau this afternoon. She is deeply unhappy about the idea of having an abortion but she doesn't want the baby. Giles is absurd. Thank God I'm well out of it. I was contemplating telephoning and abusing him but I felt it was beneath and beyond me.

Last night Doug and I went over my piece. He says I am very good, apart from the way I hold myself. He says I look a little stiff and self-conscious.

June 2nd

I've just been for the audition. Luckily I didn't wear
the big boobs although it would have been an interesting exercise. It went badly wrong. First because I
was meant to have rehearsed a part from Shakespeare
– an Ophelia, a Desdemona, a Viola, a Kate. One girl
even did Lady Macbeth. I had to admit that I had
nothing prepared. Then they asked me who had
written my modern. Everyone else had something by
Tennessee Williams, Eugene O'Neill, Arthur Miller or
Caryl Churchill.

I said I was going to do something by Douglas
Radcliffe. They looked at each other. I think for a
moment they thought they should have heard of him
and then one man with a goatee beard came out with
it and said, 'Who the hell is he?'

I said, 'A friend,' and they ummed and ahhed and
asked to look at the script. The same man who had
said who the hell is he asked me what I knew about
people with suicidal tendencies and I said I knew my
mother who was on Prozac.

We then had to do an improvisation, turn into
an animal and back again. Everyone contorted them-
selves into weird animal-like positions while I crawled
along the floor imagining that I was a centipede.

At lunch time I went to the pub with a boy called
Nick, who'd given me a light while we were both

taking a cigarette break in the corridor. He rolled a joint and we smoked it outside. He says he knows that one day he will be a big star so he doesn't really care if he gets into the drama school or not. Apparently he went to see a psychic who told him he would be a big star one day. I said I didn't care either because I had a small part in a Hollywood film. He was very impressed.

After lunch the two judges sat in on a class called Sense-Memory. We all had to lie on the floor and remember something traumatic. People started screaming and raving and one girl was so traumatised that she actually ran out of the room. I tried to remember how I'd felt when Giles shot the cat. It made me sad for a moment but then I looked over at Nick who was curled up snorting with laughter and banging his fist on the floor. I burst out laughing and tried to stop, but I couldn't, so I pretended I was crying . . . It was too painful to stop laughing, so I gave into it and we were both asked to leave the room. At the end of the day we were told that neither of us had got in.

June 3rd

I was rather depressed this morning because of the audition that went so badly wrong. Doug offered to take me to lunch and we drove to a Thai café in Chiswick. The anonymity of the place turned me on and I loved kissing his neck and holding his hand under the table. His mouth beckons me, it begs to be kissed, but it twists, now you have me, now you don't.

40

When Giancarlo telephones and asks, 'How are things?' I feel like saying, 'I'm madly in love, madly, deeply, profoundly, passionately. Perfectly. And not with you.'

Of course I don't say anything like that because I don't want to hurt his feelings.

Doug cheered me up by saying that now I don't have to pay for the acting course, we could release Edward's car. We drove to the pound in the Lots Road, right near Stella's. I paid for the car, £579, drove it out and it spluttered to a halt two hundred yards from the gates. Doug looked at it, shrugged his shoulders and said it was dead. I telephoned Edward and told him the whole story. 'Why didn't you tell me before?' he asked.

'I don't know,' I said. 'I didn't have the money to release it and I didn't want to remind you that you have a car you can't drive.'

'Leave it there,' he said, 'I'll get the AA to dump it somewhere. Look, get those tits on, finish that story and I'll give you something easy to do after that to pay for getting it out.'

God it's so easy. I should have told him right at the beginning. If only I had.

Doug and I went to Holland Park. We sat on a bench in the rose garden and discussed the horrors of our respective childhoods. I told him that when I was a child Daddy used to say, 'Piss off,' whenever I went near him on the rare occasions he was home. 'Piss off and play.' He confessed years later that he didn't like children, not even me. Stella was a distant figure,

41

always busy in the background. She hired a monster to look after me, an Irish woman who hit me and terrorised me by claiming that she had a black bird who kept watch on me when she wasn't around.

At night the shadows on the walls became menacing monsters, but I could not quell my terror by turning the light on. Turning the light was against the rules, she had warned me that the black bird would inform her if I disobeyed. I did not believe that the bird could actually speak but I thought that the Irish she-devil could understand its thoughts, the same way I communicated with my teddy bear. When I was seven this witch said, 'You're too old to sleep with teddy now.' She watched over me as I put my poor Toffee-bear into a drawer, where he remained for two years until monster-woman was dismissed after May discovered the gin bottles in her bedroom.

Doug grew up in Devon and one summer on his twelfth birthday, twelve boys were invited for tea. It was late August and after the cake had been eaten the boys played in the fields. When his father got home from work, he rounded up the boys and, red with rage, lined them up and beat them one by one with a belt. He was angry because a patch of corn had been flattened. Doug said he never celebrated another birthday, in fact his father had never mentioned his birthday again.

When he was thirteen, his father left home with Doug's younger brother, who was sent to an expensive private school. His mother was penniless, but from that day on Doug's father did not provide for his wife and elder son. His mother waitressed in a local pub and Doug worked on Saturdays mucking

42

out the stables at a riding school. When they were at home together his mother cried and cried and he would have to comfort her and hold her, wipe away her tears and sleep in her bed.

When I was a teenager Mummy became Stella the Enemy. She told me I was useless and hopeless until I believed it to be true. Once she ordered me to do the washing-up, and I rolled my eyes to the ceiling, exasperated by the loathing in her eyes. She came at me, mad and wild, and she hit me again and again around the face. The fright made me involuntarily pee. I was immobilised by the assault, I couldn't even push her away.

June 6th

My old school friend, Eloise Tartan, has come to stay. She's a model. She was engaged to a drummer in New York, but she's just found out that he's having an affair with a backing singer who was touring with the group. The wedding has been called off and she wants to move back to London. She's going to stay here until she finds somewhere else to live. Eloise is too beautiful to be true. Eloise Tartan the girl who locked the staff into the staff room at school while we gleefully missed most of double maths before an emergency locksmith arrived to set them free.

She loves the big-boobs job. She told me that if I want a reaction I am going to have to flaunt my boobs. Today she forced me into them and out to the park. 'Jog,' she screamed. 'Jog.' I laughed so much that I couldn't walk let alone job, but, desperate for something to write, I finally jogged past a group of men. 'That was big,' I heard one of them mutter.

This afternoon, we dragged Matthew to Harvey Nichols lingerie department, and while I stood in a corner, huge-boobed and embarrassed, his task was to ask the sales assistant what size bra he should buy me as a surprise. The sales assistant was meant to gasp and say 48 DD, but apparently she looked me up and down and said it was impossible to tell, she would have to measure my back.

June 20th

The news is that I am flying to LA tomorrow. Apparently I am needed now instead of the second week of July. Edward has advanced me some money for the boob piece which he thinks is very funny, so I've been able to buy my ticket, which Greg says Henry The Big Producer will reimburse.

June 21st

Doug came to pick me up last night for a goodbye dinner. I was wearing Eloise's short black dress and a pair of her kinky Prada boots. I was feeling good. I went to get my jacket and when I came back, Doug said, 'Bye Eloise, have a good evening.'

'Yeh,' she sighed, 'well, I'll be watching a repeat of *Floyd on Fish*.'

'You could come with us,' he said, glancing at me. I shot him a look *no way*, but it was too late and she said she'd love to.

We went to the River Café. Doug sat next to me and Eloise opposite him. To say she was flirting with him

44

would be a colossal understatement. She never once looked at me and at one point she smiled seductively and wiped a bit of rocket salad off his cheek with her napkin. When we got back here she came to say goodnight to us wearing nothing but a tiny towel and she kissed Doug on the lips. What she is up to I really can't think, but her behaviour really upset me, particularly as she is staying in the flat. We left early this morning, so there was no chance to talk to her.

Douglas dropped me at Heathrow in a Mercedes which was given to him by a rich patron, a divorcee. He vehemently denies that anything has ever happened between them. 'She's nearly twice my age,' he said when I asked.

'But people don't just give cars away for no reason,' I said.

'Don't they?' he laughed. 'She owns several cars, she's too rich to walk.'

'Even so,' I said, 'it seems a little strange. You must have kissed her once, or something.'

'Not true,' he said, 'although maybe she is a little obsessed with me. She hasn't got much else to think about.'

'When you get back,' he said, putting his hand on my thigh, 'let's go somewhere. Rent a flat, perhaps in Paris or Amsterdam. I want to go away and finish my script.'

Amsterdam. The last time I went to Amsterdam it was with Giles for New Year's Eve. We were staying in a grotty hotel. A bare, low-watt light bulb hung from the ceiling and there were no reading lamps by the bed. Giles The Moron had forgotten the piece of paper with his friends' telephone number

45

and address, so we never got to their New Year's Eve party which was the reason we had invested in a trip to Amsterdam in the first place.

We were talking generally about ex-lovers when Doug suddenly said, 'A man usually has many lovers unless it is the real thing.'

'How many lovers do you have?' I asked trying to sound light and carefree.

'Only you sweetie,' he said picking up my hand and kissing it. Then he laughed. 'For the moment.'

I laughed too, but a wave of uneasiness flooded through me and settled. I wanted to ask, 'What will happen between us? How long will we be together? Do you love me?'

I'm writing this on the plane. I still feel uneasy, but I can't stop thinking about his hands and his mouth and the way his skin is so golden.

June 22nd

The sun shines but nothing else seems to. Everything is so big, the avenues are so wide, the cars huge, but there is a down-at-heel feel, an after-the-party *ambiance*. I'm staying in a small house in Beverly Hills, with Nancy, a friend of Henry The Big Producer's. She's a casting director and she's forty, thin and single, and desperate to move to New York. She's paranoid about everything and particularly about living in LA. She's worried about being mugged or being wiped out by an earthquake or shot down by the gun-wielding gangs down-town.

She says that no one with any sense will go down-town after sunset. 'If your car breaks down

46

there, you've had it,' she told me. I understand there must be some kind of a problem in LA, but I do think it is slightly excessive to hire a private policeman to guard the property and to have not one but three signs in her garden saying Armed Response.

We drove in her pink, open-topped, Cadillac to the Beverly Wilshire Hotel. She's having a lettuce-leaf lunch here, while I am lying by the pool. It's all a bit disappointing. I was expecting LA to be packed with shiny petrol stations and brightly-coloured boards, but everything is dusty and faded. There is a blonde girl reading next to me who looks remarkably like a recent Bond girl. She is probably going to get someone to page her, so she can walk across to the telephone in her designer bathing suit and be rediscovered by a producer: maybe the man sitting opposite me who is eating a triple-decked club sandwich.

I'm now back at the house. I've just spoken to Henry Irving's secretary and she told me I have to be at the studio tomorrow at 7.00 a.m. I told her that I hadn't seen a script yet and she said, don't worry about a thing. I called Greg collect and said, 'You're my agent, now what is going on?'

'Nothing is going on,' he said. 'You have a three-week contract, $200 a day.'

'But,' I said, 'I don't know what part I'm playing, I haven't been able to learn my lines.'

'You're one of the schoolgirls,' he told me. 'It's a small part, you can learn the lines on the set.'

I'm worried. First because of the part, secondly because Nancy is taking me to a party tonight in Santa Monica and I won't know a soul, and thirdly because

Eloise has probably turned up naked at Doug's door by now.

June 23rd

The party was by a poolside. There was a buffet of lobster, crab salad, couscous and caviar. I was helping myself to a salad when a huge lobster – the one who got away – crawled to the edge of the table. I screamed and everyone looked round at me. After that I couldn't eat a thing so I drank a couple of margaritas and then a couple more and finally my head was spinning.

Henry The Big Producer arrived and Nancy took me over to say hello. He looked harassed and preoccupied as usual. He introduced me to a few people, but all the time he was looking over my shoulder, checking to see if there was a more important person hovering nearby whom he should be talking to. I admit I was scanning the room too. I longed to see Jack Nicholson or Gary Oldman or Ralph Fiennes, but the only recognisable face was that actor Jeff Goldblum who once starred as a fly and appears in all those beer ads. I drank another couple of margarita's before I suddenly realised I was going to be sick.

I rushed through the crowd and managed to make it to a turquoise bathroom en suite to a yellow bedroom. I lay down on the cold, marble floor. After a while there was a knock and a woman asked if I was OK. I couldn't reply. Five minutes later she knocked again. I staggered to the door and let her in. 'My God,' she said, 'you're as white as a

48

sheet. Wait there. Don't move. I'll be back. I'll knock twice.' When she returned she handed me a bottle of Perrier.

'Thank you,' I said weakly.

I sprayed water from the shower head all over my neck and head and then flopped down on to the loo seat. The woman said, 'Do you mind?', pointing at the loo, and hitching up her dress. When she had finished she went straight to the mirror, pouted her lips, applied a bright red lipstick and then stood back to get a fuller picture. 'My noo pair. Aren't they great?' she said, squeezing her breasts. I looked at her through a nauseous haze and then she pulled her dress right up to her neck.

'Fabulous,' I muttered, before lifting the loo seat and throwing up again.

I arrived at the studio at seven, feeling hungover, dehydrated and tired. I reported to a woman who had long, frizzy hennaed hair down to her waist. She asked me who I was and then looked down a list and said, 'Scene 22, midnight feast,' and sent me off to get my costume and make-up. A man wearing about fourteen studs in one ear and purple lycra bicycling shorts handed me a tiny nightdress. I asked for a dressing-gown and he gave me some kind of a towelling thing.

After make-up I was left with a group of girls, dressed in nightdresses who all seemed to know each other. 'Are you really English?' one of them asked me.

'Yes,' I said. 'Who is who? Do you know who I am playing?'

'Oh we're all extras,' she said. 'We're the girls.

Today we are all in the midnight feast scene, throwing pillows around. Maybe you'll get a line, if you've come all the way from England.' It began to sink in, the reason that no one has sent me a script and everyone had been so vague.

I went to search for Henry. I asked a technician where he was and he told me to go to the production office, which is where I found him, talking to the director. He nodded at me. I waited for ages, shifting from foot to foot. Eventually he turned around. 'Um,' I said, 'I didn't realise I was an extra. I thought I had a part. I mean I thought you had offered me a part and that is why I came here.'

'A part?' He looked incredulous. 'I pulled a few strings getting you this far, and that's because I owed that, what's his name, Greg, a favour. He said you wanted to be in the movie. We hired you as an extra. You don't have experience as an actress. We can't just give you a role, like that honey.'

'Right,' I said. 'But do you think I'll get a line?'

'Perhaps,' he said, lighting a cigar. 'Now if you'll excuse me I have another angry person waiting to talk to me.'

That was it then. Duped. It could have been worse. I could have been dumped in a soft porn movie and at least I'm earning money. But jumping around in a negligee? I sat down and lit a cigarette, and the frizzy PR girl came up to me and said, 'Scene 22, ten minutes, no smoking in the studio.'

The midnight feast scene was absurd. All the girls were much too old and the dialogue was far too dated, like something out of an Enid Blyton book. The British accents were strange. Winona Ryder who plays the lead was good, but some of the other girls sounded like something out of *Brief Encounter*. My job was to say, 'Look girls, I've got some toffee.'

June 24th

I'm employed for another four weeks. The PA girl gave me a copy of a script, which I had to nag and beg for. I've gone through the whole thing. The script is really not that funny or authentic. I'm sitting here in the studio, it's 2.00 p.m. and we've been hanging around since 7.30 a.m. this morning.

Nancy invited me to dinner last night at a French restaurant called Café des Artistes and one of the executive producers from the movie joined us. He's from Newcastle and he's called Stewart. I told him that I had spent a short time at an English boarding school. He asked me what it was like, and whether the movie captured the essence of boarding school life. That set me off on a roll. I said that although girls in Enid Blyton novels were endlessly having midnight feasts, in real life girls at boarding schools over the age of twelve never do. They may get up in the middle of the night to smoke cigarettes and drink a bottle of vodka, but they would never throw pillows around and say things like golly gosh, whiz and super.

'Interesting,' he said. 'Very interesting.'

Doug rang early this morning. He said he was missing me and that he was going to fax me an outline of a film he has in mind. He wants me to show it to Henry Irving.

Brilliant. That man Stewart just came by and said he was interested in what I had to say last night

51

and that he'd like to meet me tomorrow morning for breakfast at 6.00 a.m.!

June 25th

We met in a diner. Hash browns and eggs over easy. The waitresses' uniforms were crumpled and the cutlery was cloudy. I talked at length about boarding school life, and boarding school language. He asked me if I wanted to continue as an extra and I didn't want to appear surly, so I said I was happy to fulfil my contract but it wasn't what I had been expecting and then he said, well perhaps we could hire you as a script consultant instead.

'My God,' I said, 'I'd love to. To be honest, acting as a background schoolgirl isn't really my thing.'

Doug sent me a fax today with the outline of a treatment for the film he wants me to show Henry Irving. It made me laugh. He can't possibly be serious but I think he is.

This is the tragic story of a young Finnish writer, schizophrenic and suicidal, paralysed by his love for his blind half-sister. When she miraculously regains her sight and promptly rejects him he sets out on a Hungerford-style massacre of a local fishing village.

June 26th

Stewart telephoned this morning and confirmed that he was offering me work as a script consultant at $150 an hour! I gulped on the telephone, and he said, 'We feel you have much more to offer us in this capacity.' I am so pleased, and excited, because extra work is soul-destroying, particularly having to wear those short gym slips and negligees.

Today I went for a meeting with Stewart, a couple of writers and another woman. We talked for a long time. The two writers and the woman were taking notes, which gave me a real thrill. The writers were very interested in the boarding school lingo that I reeled off. 'Bilglab' for biology laboratory, 'lax' for lacrosse, 'bog' for loo, and 'vains infinity' for 'I'll never do that for as long as I live.' 'Old bag' for ugly old housemistress, 'bag' as in 'that place is saved for my friend' and 'pipping' as in 'I am pipped on Polly,' meaning I have a crush on Polly.

There was a long conversation about what brand of cigarettes the girls should smoke. In my day there was a horrible brand called Number Six, which were smaller and cheaper than other brands. We called them Shit Six. Stewart wants to choose the brand that will offer the most cash, which in the film business is known as product placement.

The writers were quite interested in incorporating a story of a schoolgirl crush. It's traditional in all girls' English boarding schools for the younger girls to have crushes on the older ones. There is no sex involved. It's more like courtly love. The older girl is worshipped from afar. Younger girls blush and giggle when the object of their adoration passes them and sometimes the braver ones ambush their chosen goddess with a note or a bag of sweets.

At the end of the session I showed Stewart Doug's fax and he laughed and asked whether it was for real.

53

July 7th

I'm flying back to London and I am exhausted. This is the first moment I have had to write. I've earned about twelve thousand dollars, which is not bad for ten days' work. It's brilliant, it's the business. I'm desperate to see Doug, dying to, although I was slightly perturbed by that ridiculous outline he faxed. I managed to leave a copy of it with one of Henry The Big Producer's secretaries. I felt I had to.

My God I feel sick with nerves and disappointment. Doug was waiting for me at Heathrow. I hugged him and kissed him and he smiled at me. I was high on being with him but then I got into his Mercedes and crashed down to earth. There on the floor was one of Eloise's leopard skin gloves. I didn't say anything for a while, because I was so upset. 'What's the matter, baby?' he asked at last. I picked up the glove. He looked at me and laughed.

'What was she doing in here?' I asked.

'Who?'

'Eloise. That's her glove,' I said coldly.

'Nothing,' he said, giggling nervously. 'Last week I bumped into her and gave her a lift to a studio.'

I wanted to believe him. I don't know why, but I didn't and it was impossible for me to talk to him, or look at him. When he dropped me at my door I fled from the car and mumbled goodbye.

Maria was at home, wearing my black jacket, but there was no sign of Eloise. It was my turn to sob. 'What has happened?' she asked.

'What's been going on with Eloise?' I asked.

54

'Has she been seeing Doug?'

Maria looked embarrassed. 'You have to tell me,' I beseeched her. 'It's making me feel crazy.' She said she had heard Doug's voice on the intercom and a couple of times on the answering machine. 'Did he ever stay here?'

'No he never stay here,' she said, 'but to tell you the truth, I heard him leaving one message for Eloise arranging a weekend away together. Eloise did go away last weekend and he came to pick her up on Friday night. That is when I heard his voice on the intercom and buzzed him in.'

It was like a horror story. How could he? And Eloise, she knows I'm mad about him. Stealing a girlfriend's boyfriend is taboo, an unwritten rule that I never thought she would break when it came down to it. I'll never forgive her. And I'm obviously not the 'real thing' in Doug's life, but I suspected that when he dropped me off at the airport.

I telephoned Giancarlo. I haven't spoken to him since I left for America. He was a bit whiney at first, he was grieved that he hadn't known where to contact me. 'All I know is Los Angeles,' he said. 'Somewhere in Los Angeles.'

I began to give him a frothy account of what had happened to me and then I burst into tears. 'What is it?' he asked me. 'What?'

'Oh nothing,' I said, 'a touch of jet lag.'

July 8th

Doug obviously contacted Eloise because she hasn't dared show her face here. I counted twenty-four pairs of her shoes. I put the left-footed shoes (including the Prada boot) in a suitcase and then ran into the street. I was very hyped up about what I was going to do. I hailed a taxi and asked the driver to take me to the nearest bridge with water underneath. He took me to the Great Western Road and we stopped by the canal. Imagine his astonishment when I hurled the bag of left-footed shoes into the murky water.

Eloise came back this evening. Imagine her embarrassment.

'Hi,' she said, moving forward to kiss me.

I was ice. 'You'd better go,' was all I managed to say. I went to the bathroom and began to run a bath. She knocked but I pretended I couldn't hear over the running water.

'Anna,' she said, 'Anna.'

'I know about you and Doug,' I shouted. 'So go away.'

'Please listen, it didn't mean anything.'

I opened the door and said quite calmly, 'If it didn't mean anything, why the hell do it?'

'I don't know,' she said, 'but I'd like to stay and make it up with you.'

'Go to Doug's.'

'He's a bastard,' she said, 'a bastard. He won't talk to me.'

'I feel very sorry for you,' I said. 'I really do.' Then I smiled mysteriously, because I was thinking about the twenty-four left-footed boots and shoes, rotting at the bottom of the muddy canal.

July 9th

Douglas telephoned this morning. 'Hi,' he said.

I said nothing. I was waiting for him to continue, wondering what he would say.

'Look, I know you don't want to talk to me at the moment, but I just wanted to say, that I'm here for you if you want to get in touch. It was a mistake, a frivolous escapade. A bit of fun. I was missing you, baby.'

'Fun to go off with one of my friends,' I said. 'Fun! I wasn't real enough for you, not the real thing.'

'Anna. Let's talk later,' he said, 'when you have calmed down.'

'Let's not,' I said. 'I am perfectly calm,' I said, 'calm enough to know that I don't want to see you ever again.'

'OK,' he said. 'But you can change your mind, I'm here.'

He left a message this afternoon: 'By the way, any news about my treatment?'

He telephoned again, when I was in the middle of waxing my legs. 'What?' I said.

'My treatment? Any news?'

'Your treatment. Your treatment of women is appalling. Your schizophrenic drama treatment is comical. I've left it with Henry Irving. He'll have a good laugh, no doubt, and then call you.'

'Very funny,' he said. 'You know it's not a comedy.'

'Isn't it?' I said. 'What is it then?'

July 16th

I have been a recluse since the Doug and Eloise drama and Maria has been very subdued since her abortion last week. We are a fun pair. She lies in bed watching daytime television and smoking menthol cigarettes through a plastic filter while I mooch around flicking through car magazines, wondering vaguely if I should buy a car with the money I made in LA. I never told Greg about being hired as a consultant at $150 an hour because he would have squeezed me for whatever percentage he felt due to him, which as far as I am concerned is nought per cent. Stewart said he would arrange to have my cheque sent to Greg, invoiced as 'Extra – $200 per day'. The balance will be sent direct to me.

Last week I waited on Maria hand and foot and tried to keep the flat reasonably tidy, but I'm not that good at cleaning. She made me swear not to tell GC about the abortion. We had a plot worked out in case he arrived unexpectedly. We were going to say that Maria had a strange virus, although it never would have worked. Giancarlo would have been on to his secretary to book appointments with every specialist in the land.

July 18th

Unbearable heat. Hot hot hot and impossible to sleep. I spent the night pacing, smoking, sighing, tossing, turning and slugging flat water from a plastic bottle. I finally slept at about six in the morning, but woke a couple of hours later. I was dying for a cup of tea, but unfortunately there was no milk. In fact there was nothing in the fridge apart from an almost empty bottle of white wine and quarter of a tub of humous. It was too depressing to bear. I put on one of Giancarlo's huge jumpers and quite calmly crept downstairs and nicked Ivan Greenberg's red-topped bottle of milk from the doorstep.

Ivan Greenberg lives on the top floor. He's a property man and he owns a white Aston Martin. 'Can never be too sure,' he said to me the other day, locking a tortuous looking instrument on to the steering wheel and then putting what can only be described as a clamp on to the back wheel. 'This car is worth £28,000, the stereo alone cost me £2,000. Even the speakers are worth a grand.'

'I suppose you could keep it in a garage.'

'Yes I could, if I had the space. I do rent a garage but two of my more valuable cars are parked in there. Would you like to take a look?'

'Oh I don't think so,' I said, glancing at my watch. 'There are one or two things I should be doing.'

'They're right here,' he said, pulling a couple of Polaroids out of his top pocket. They looked like cars from a science fiction movie, or something that Batman might use on his day off.

'Great,' I said, thinking they were hideous and

59

that I would never be seen dead in one. 'What are they?'

'What are they?' He looked incredulous. 'You don't know what they are . . . ?'

'No,' I said, yawning. Ferraris I think he said.

July 19th

Today I received a four-page letter from Douglas written in the third person: Please excuse him for being so difficult with her etc. He is so sorry to upset her. He is unused to emotional stability. He is holed up in Cornwall, where he hopes to stay for a month, finishing his script. At the end he signed: On his behalf Douglas.

Although my stomach dived when I recognised the writing on the envelope the actual letter was really too much. How could he be so pretentious? I showed the letter to Beatrice. She thinks he may be schizophrenic. We discussed the possibility that he may be mad, after all thinking one has a dual personality is definitely a sign of madness.

Ivan Greenberg rang the doorbell last night. 'I was wondering if you knew anything about a certain missing bottle?'

'Bottle?' I asked, eyes widening. 'No. What kind of bottle?'

'A red-topped bottle of milk, which was stolen this morning from outside the front door. I have a bottle of milk and a carton of orange juice delivered every morning.'

'Do you? Can you get orange juice delivered? How brilliant, do they deliver anything else?'

'I really don't know,' he said, 'but if you happen to find out anything about my milk please let me know.'

'Of course, Ivan.'

'Thank you.' He turned abruptly.

I called after him and asked his advice on where I could get a reasonably priced car. His demeanour changed at once. He became animated, and even asked for a pen and wrote down the address of a garage in Fulham. He advised me to talk to a man named James and told me to mention his name.

July 24th

Drama. Beatrice and Sapphire arranged a surprise birthday party for me a couple of nights ago at Giancarlo's flat. I was really excited that day, adrenalin rushing and all that, because I had gone to Ivan's garage and bought myself the ultimate present, a car of my own. A Ford with power steering and a sun-roof. Stella invited me over at drinks time and gave me a watch she had picked up at an antique market and I was amazed to find a card from Dad with a cheque enclosed for £50.

When I returned to the flat there were about thirty people singing 'Happy Birthday to You' as I walked through the door. It was really exciting, particularly as I didn't even know half the guests. Sweet Sapphire had organised a cake with candles and she turned off the lights and brought it in. Everyone was dancing, singing and clapping when Maria tugged at my arm and introduced me to Giancarlo's brother, Roberto, who introduced me to a woman who can only be described as an Ivana Trump clone. It was such a shock, because I wasn't even aware that Giancarlo had a brother.

Roberto is smaller than Giancarlo and has lost more hair, but he has a jollier disposition. 'So sorry,' he said, 'everything is last second. Giancarlo said we

62

could use the flat this weekend. I think he probably left a message for you.'

'No, I don't think so,' I said. 'Well maybe. I haven't listened to my messages for a while. I hope you don't mind there are a few people here celebrating my birthday.'

'Fantastic. Happy birthday,' he said, kissing me on both cheeks. 'You know,' he said, raising his voice above the music, 'this is incredible. You have a birthday today, and my birthday was last week. We are both Cancers. Isn't that a big, fantastic coincidence.'

They followed me through the throng of swaying bodies. Roberto was carrying two suitcases but managed to dance along at the same time. Ivana held on to him in congo mode. I showed them to Giancarlo's bedroom, but the bed was strewn with coats and amid the pile Rosie Wheaton was lying there with a man I didn't know. He seemed to be smoking a joint with one hand and groping her breast with another. They smiled at us, and the man removed his hand from her breast and gave us a languid wave.

'So many gatecrashers,' I said, ushering Ivana and Roberto out. I took them to my room. At least the bed was made, but I had to quickly scoop up three pairs of dirty knickers that lay on the floor.

Much later on in the evening Roberto and Ivana were dancing slowly, locked in a tight embrace when a man laden down with cameras appeared from nowhere and snapped a few shots at them, the flash flashing dramatically. Roberto lashed out and chased him out and there was a scuffle outside. Ivana rushed to the bedroom and Roberto returned looking ruffled and distraught.

What we didn't know at the time is that Ivana is the wife of an eminent and powerful Italian politician. I just can't think who tipped off a photographer, unless they were followed from the airport. The next morning a photograph was splashed on the front page of the *Sun*. Ivana, with her arms wrapped around Roberto's neck, kissing him passionately as if for the last time.

The same morning we were under siege and it was terrifying. A seething crowd of journalists and photographers gathered outside on the pavement and at first we didn't know why. When Maria returned with the paper the awful truth was revealed. Poor Roberto and Ivana, they were so freaked out. Even though Giancarlo is ex-directory, the phone began to ring mid-morning and the journo-rats were sniffing at the other end.

I unplugged the telephone and then we had to plan their getaway as there was no way they were going to be able to slide out of the front door incognito. In the end we decided the only possible exit route was from the balcony. If we could get a ladder they would be able to climb down into the communal gardens. Of course it would be easier to escape from the ground floor and basement flat, but unfortunately the couple are away. Poor Matthew Clivesmith was hauled in to help, which is very kind of him as he arrived in his lunch hour disguised as a window cleaner and carrying a ladder.

Greg sent a fax late afternoon because the telephone was still off the hook. 'Call me. How about that piece in the *Sun*?' By the time I telephoned, I was coming down off the drama, rather hungover and very near to tears. Greg was very sweet and sympathetic and rushed over to see me with a box of chocolate éclairs. 'So where are the star-crossed lovers now? What are their plans?' he asked when he arrived. I told him that I had no idea.

Giancarlo arrived that evening, having fought his way through the diminished crowd of hard-core tabloid terrorists who were the only ones who had bothered to remain huddled outside the front door. Maria and I were still clearing up from the party when he arrived and we were both shattered. Giancarlo was very agitated. He is convinced that the photograph will have huge repercussions, both politically and personally. He thinks the minister may have to resign and he is worried that Roberto may be assassinated as he is certain that the minister is backed by Mafia money. I tried to calm him down, to say it was very unlikely that anything dramatic will happen to his brother.

'You never told me it was your birthday,' he whined, refusing to let the subject drop. He went on and on. I tried to tell him that I hadn't expected to celebrate my birthday. He seemed put out that I had partied without him, and that he had not been responsible for organising something for me himself.

He went back to New York yesterday. There was another blow-up when he found drug paraphernalia in his bedroom, some tobacco and roaches, a bag of grass, and a bit of silver foil stained in brown lines that someone had used to smoke heroin. Luckily I don't think he knew what the silver foil was used for, but he understood the general druggy message. He's calmed down but he thinks I need to see a shrink.

July 27th

I woke up this morning to find the fridge nearly empty. I sneaked down to the front door and nicked Ivan's red-topped bottle again. While I was furtively snatching it, I got the familiar feeling of stampeding adrenalin causing a tightening and fizzing in the head and a leaping of the heart. I remember this sensation from the days when Sapphire and I used to shoplift.

The little nerd caught me red-handed when I was creeping back up the stairs with the bottle sticking out of my dressing-gown pocket. He was wearing leggings and trainers, ready for a jog. 'You must be frightfully embarrassed,' he said.

'No,' I said, blushing. 'Actually I was bringing the bottle up for you, I went down to see if a letter I was expecting had arrived.'

'Really?' he said, taking the bottle from my hand. 'Pigs will fly.'

We were standing outside my front door when I realised the awful truth. Maria had taken the night off to visit a friend at language college in Oxford and I had locked myself out. Punished for my sins. There was nothing for it, but to beg for mercy and refuge. 'Come on,' he said smugly, 'I suppose you'd better come up to my apartment.'

His wide, spongy bum, the short legs in the maroon lycra trousers, the balding shining circle at the back of his head . . . How I hated him. When he opened his front door, a stale, unsensual
66

smell pervaded. The sitting room was like a dentist's waiting room with old car magazines spread over a low glass table. There was a carriage clock on the mantelpiece and one or two out-of-date invitations propped up rather desperately. 'Now you can call a locksmith, but I don't want you to touch anything while I am out,' he said as I picked up a tapestried cushion – a kitsch design of a kitten playing with a ball of pink wool.

As soon as he'd gone I went into the small narrow kitchen. There was a loaf of curling white sandwich bread in the bread bin and a packet of plain digestives. In the fridge there was a small bottle of fresh out-of-date orange juice, a tin of rollmops, half a packet of cheddar wrapped in crumpled silver foil, two cans of low-alcohol beer and the offending bottle of milk.

The bedroom was depressing. Brown walls clashed with a brown bedspread. On the bedside table there was a radio alarm, a bottle of aspirin, a property magazine and a novel by Jeffrey Archer. I rummaged around in the drawer looking for a porn mag or a packet of condoms but there was nothing except a checked handkerchief and a small comb with several teeth missing.

August 2nd

Today I spent two hours looking for my car. It was very humiliating because Ivan caught me wandering around outside. 'What have you lost?' he asked. 'Your keys again?'

'No my car actually.'

'You'll lose your brain next,' he laughed nervously. He seemed delighted to be proved right that I am a thieving, flakey, babe.

I telephoned the police and the council but it hadn't been towed away. It was Maria who suggested that perhaps it had been stolen. Stolen. My new second-hand car with the go-faster stripes, my pride and joy. It seemed hardly possible, but I reported it to the police anyway. I have a heavy heart. Surely this is bad karma, meaning that this has happened because I stole Ivan's milk.

August 3rd

Sapphire, her new boyfriend, Big John, and I are going to Gloucestershire to stay with May next weekend. I can't wait to get out of London and see her. May lives with a philosophy professor whom she met on a walking tour in the Spanish Pyrenees. She has a slight penchant for professors, her first ever love affair was with her English professor at Oxford. They eloped when she was nineteen. The professor, who was thirty-five, was considered a much older man.

She's never married. I've heard people say the love of her life was a man she met in her late thirties, but the affair ended abruptly when she was in her mid-forties. She writes intriguing poetry and she's had a few volumes published. Her themes are about missed opportunities, bad timing and misunderstanding. The sadness and confusion of love.

It is said that in her day, May was a *femme fatale* and broke many hearts. It is also rumoured that the house she lives in, Waterstone House in the village of Waterstone, was given to her by one of her lovers which provoked the man's son to begin a law-suit which was eventually dropped.

The strangest thing has just happened. A policeman telephoned saying his name was Detective Tom Roberts from the Flying Squad, Tower Bridge. 'We 'ave your car,' he said.

'Oh great,' I said. 'Can I come and pick it up?'

'Not quite yet, you see it's not a simple case. We have to check it out, you can pick it up this evening.'

'What do you mean, not a simple case?'

'Come down to the station tonight and I'll explain all.'

God, I thought, I wonder what the hell is going on?

August 6th

Detective Tom Roberts is cute and cockney, with short, dark, spiky hair, quite a large nose and luscious lips. He was wearing cool-blue Levi's and a black, beaten-up leather jacket. He shook my hand

69

and then led me to a yard behind the station where my car with the go-faster stripes was parked rather humbly next to a silver BMW. I blurted something out about having an out-of-date tax disc, but the detective dismissed me, as if to say that tax discs like lost dogs are matters best left to young uniformed policemen who work in a labyrinth of ill-lit rooms behind lowly desks, somewhere far away.

'Anything missing?' He asked the question as though he knew and was testing me.

'A Sheryl Crow tape?' I said hesitantly. He laughed.

'The bloke – used your cheque-book.'

'My *cheque-book*?'

'Yeh, it was left in the car.'

'Was it?'

'Yeh.'

'Oh yes.' Had I left it there? I knew that if I didn't pull myself together and appear more responsible, unless I stopped behaving like a throwaway flakey babe, he would lose interest in the case. 'Yes you're right, there was a cheque-book in the car,' I said quickly.

I then worried that he was going to add that the car had not been locked. 'One of the easiest cars to break into, Fords,' he said, somehow picking up my thoughts and deciding to save me. 'Although I can't think why anyone would want one,' he was grinning at me, challenging.

'Steady on,' I said, realising that he had quite suddenly overstepped the limits of professionalism and was now entering the realms of flirtation.

'And I don't know wevfar you've noticed the spare tyre in the back there.'

70

'Oh yes,' I said, wondering what he was talking about.

He was getting it out for me and putting it back in the boot. 'The scum-bag used that as collateral, when 'e wanted some petrol an' didn't 'av the money to pay. 'E tried to pay wif one of your cheques, said you was his wife, but the Pakistani at the garage wasn't sure he could accept it wivou' a card. 'Is boss was away, so scum-bag left your tyre and said he would be back. When we picked 'im up, 'e confessed everyfing, was very co-operative. We retraced 'is steps, got the tyre back and a couple of cheques.'

'Thank you,' I said, thinking that what little tax I have ever paid is definitely being put to good use, paying people like Tom to chase after my spare tyres and missing cheques, but I rather wished that something more exciting had happened, for example a couple of dead bodies or a great stash of drugs had been found in the boot.

He then explained that the man who had stolen my car was an escaped convict who has been under surveillance for the last two months because the police were tipped-off that he was part of a ring of security-van thieves who were planning a big heist. It was obviously a waste of time to rearrest him for stealing my car so they received special dispensation from the Home Office to keep him under surveillance and not inform me that my car had been found. Soon it became apparent that the man was just a boring old junkie and his drug habit was out of control. He was never going to do anything more than fix himself up, buy some cakes and chocolate for the sugar trip that

71

junkies yearn and go off and score all over again.

I sat in a small room with the detective for two hours, filling in form after form. He sighed and told me that he is more used to dealing with armed criminals than paperwork, although by then I knew he wasn't just a brain-dead copper with a truncheon. When I'd finished he said he would have to keep my cheque-book until all the cheques had been accounted for.

'When can I get it back?' I asked.

'I'll bring it over,' he said, looking directly at me. 'If you invite me out to lunch.' I smiled and looked at the floor, there was something about him that made me feel coy and feminine, silly and flaky, helpless and vulnerable.

By this time, he had taken off his jacket and rolled up his sleeves. His forearms were large and muscular with just the right amount of hair. He was the kind of man who would hoist up a woman and carry her over his shoulder to bed. 'Nice looking girl like you,' he said, 'living in 'olland Park and all, whadyafink you're doing wiv that bloody Ford anyway, it doesn't suit you.' I giggled.

It was too hard to explain that it was only by a strange twist or quirk of fate that I happened to meet Giancarlo at the time that I was desperate to find somewhere to live and that he happened to have an empty flat in Holland Park that he had invited me to stay in. It was too complicated to explain that a Ford was all I could afford. I looked at him: he was smiling and scrutinising me and I thought, maybe, just maybe ... but bashfulness made me lower my eyes, which fell on his left hand. Where a fat gold wedding ring glinted under the strip light.

August 9th

We are here in Gloucestershire staying with May. Tomorrow, Sapphire, Big John, and I are going to Skara Brae's wedding.

We were having supper when May said, 'Well, what's been happening to you?' She was looking at me. This is the key-question for a game called Great Exaggerations which we usually play in front of bemused guests.

'Oh God, it's been hectic,' I said. 'A major political scandal erupted at my birthday party. Giancarlo's brother, Roberto, was caught with his mistress, who happened to be the Italian prime minister's wife and within moments it was all over the papers and even on national television news.'

'Caught? Caught by whom?'

'By the tabloid press. I still can't think how they knew. Anyway Roberto is probably going to be murdered at any moment by the Mafia. But that is not all. My car was stolen by a dangerous escaped criminal, a serial killer who was being followed by MI5 and MI6. The case was discussed in parliament and at the Home Office.'

'How riveting,' May said. Sapphire sniggered in the corner.

'The Prime Minister nearly resigned over it,' Sapphire said. 'He wanted Anna's car to be given back,
74

but the Home Office said it was more important to continue to follow him and nab him on a bigger crime.'

'He was also involved in a huge international drug ring,' I said.

'Vast,' Sapphire said. 'Controlled by Triad-like gangs.'

'Bigger than anything of the kind anyone has ever seen in this country.'

'In Europe,' Sapphire said.

'In the world,' said May, smiling wryly.

August 11th

The wedding never happened. We were all dressed up and drove in a mad rush to get there on time. We got lost about three times and ended up in a muddy field once or twice. When we arrived at the church, no one was there. 'Are you sure it's today?' I asked Sapphire.

'Yeh,' she said vaguely.

'Come on, Saff,' said Big J. 'This is as dead as a graveyard.'

'Well you thought it was today,' she said to me.

'Yes I thought it was today, because you told me it was today.'

'You mean I'm dressed up in this garb for no reason?' Big J was rolling a cigarette.

'It's probably on September 10th,' said Sapphire helpfully.

'My neighbour would love the fact that I went to a non-existent wedding,' I said, on the way back. 'He thinks I am the flakiest babe around.'

'Babe,' said Big J, 'I don't think so. Babes are just out of the wood, if you know what I mean.'

Yesterday we sunbathed by the river and gave each other foot massages, while Sapphire's twelve-year-old brother, Roddy, skipped stones on the water. This afternoon we lay on the lawn flicking through the Sunday papers and drinking tall glasses of Pimms and lemonade. A woodcock was cocking, the sun was still shining, Roddy walked towards us across the lawn. His attenuated shadow looked like the Etruscan sculpture of an elongated boy, which Giancarlo and I saw in the town of Volterra when we were driving through Tuscany the other day.

I mentioned this to the others and Big J put on an Italian accent and said something like, 'How bellissima to drive through the Italian countryside, taking in the odd bit of culture. How perfect, and by the way I would compare the effect of shadow and light on the lawn to Rembrandt's "Nightwatch", which I happened to catch the other day as I sped through Amsterdam on my way to Monte Carlo.'

I giggled although Sapphire sighed and muttered 'God' under her breath and then said 'God,' again, louder, at which point Big J said, 'Anything the matter?' and she said, 'Yes, actually. I thought what Anna said was very interesting and I happen to find shadows fascinating.' And then to emphasise the point she made Roddy do various cartwheels and handstands and had him hopping backwards and forwards so that we could study the shadow effect.

Big J asked if anyone wanted to play croquet but we shook our heads. Even Roddy said he would rather lie on the grass. We were all dulled but oddly compelled by the articles in the style sections of the papers, with titles like, 'Kiss and Make Up . . .' Does a furious row lead to a night of hot passion? Big J stomped off to play on his own. The distant hollow putt of the croquet mallet complemented the Pimms, the shadowy lawn and May's straw sun-hat with the pink satin ribbon twisted around the brim.

May was sitting in a deck-chair, absorbed by something white she was knitting. 'What are you knitting?' Big John asked her politely on his return.

'Oh nothing,' she said, 'I just like to keep my hands busy, and while we are on the subject of questions, why on earth are you called Big John?'

Big John blushed, and Sapphire giggled. I snorted while May smiled mischievously and asked the professor to bring her a small sherry with ice.

August 13th

It's depressing to see Sapphire with Big J. He's such a boorish, insecure, and chippy oik. She tells me they have something going in bed, but hopefully that won't be enough to sustain a long relationship. The drive back from Gloucestershire was a nightmare. Big J inched close to the rear end of any car blocking his way and then flashed the lights and hooted the horn until the driver was forced to change lane. Sapphire sat in the front, staring out of the side window. Big J rapped his hands against the steering wheel and sang along to his demo-tape – loud, tuneless and moronic metal.

I got back to find Maria wearing the black, lacy shirt that I bought one Saturday afternoon from Spitalfields market. I was tense from the harrowing journey and said something sharp and accusatory. She defended herself by telling me that a cousin had died and she was in mourning and had nothing black to wear.

Giancarlo has been staying here since Sunday night. He holds me with a tight rein which drives me a little crazy. Yesterday after a fairly strenuous session of stretching, twisting, balancing and breathing in a yoga class, I was enjoying the relaxation at the end, when someone came in to tell me I had a telephone call.

'It's me,' he said. 'How is everything?'

'Who?'

'Me. Giancarlo. Who else knows where you are?'

'No one. No one else is that interested in the minutiae of my daily movements.'

'How are you? You looked tired this morning.'

'Did I? Well I'm fine. Fine,' I said. 'Although I've coughed once since I saw you three hours ago.'

'Really?' he said. 'Poor you.'

'Giancarlo, unless there is anything else, I really must get back to the class. Right now.'

He's worried because his partner in New York has lost quite a large sum of money on a dud deal and his mother is ill. I know that I should be there for him, but it's impossible for me to move forward when he is standing there all the time, on my case, in my hair, and not picking up on my ironic remarks.

August 15th

When I got back last night, quite late, I found Giancarlo and a blonde girl, sitting next to each other on the sofa. The girl was very pretty, and she wore a backless simple white dress and high, elegant, sandles. They had obviously just been out for dinner. He introduced me to the girl, but he didn't stand up and kiss me like he usually does. I sat down, and felt a bolt of jealousy. He was paying her far more attention than me. For example he lit her cigarette, but he didn't light mine. I sat there and I sat it out. At last she got up, and said she had to go. Giancarlo helped her on with her jacket and left with her to look for a cab. He was out for a long time and for one hot panicky moment I imagined that they had gone home together and I didn't like it. Not one bit.

When he returned, he said goodnight and walked straight by me. I followed him into his bedroom and asked him if anything was wrong. He said that he was tired and worried about his mother and then he sat down and sighed and put his head in his hands. I went to him and gave his shoulders a massage. 'That's wonderful,' he said.

I fetched some aromatherapy oil from my bedroom, lay him down and gave his back a good, long treatment.

'Stay here with me tonight,' he said when I had finished. Now that he was offering himself to me, the idea of staying with him made me feel panicky and I hesitated. 'Just sleep here with me,' he said, 'that's all.'

I changed into a pair of his pyjamas and then we curled up together in his huge bed and he stroked my forehead until I fell asleep. In the middle of the night, I woke feeling warm and sensuous and he was awake, stroking me in all the right places, but when we finally made love it was all over in three hot, sticky, seconds and afterwards I couldn't sleep because he was snoring. I woke up in the morning feeling hungover and apprehensive, disorientated and dehydrated. I got myself a glass of water and staggered back to bed and fell asleep. By the time I woke again, Giancarlo had gone but he had left me a love note, with instructions to contact his secretary if there was anything I needed and signed with a heart crossed with an arrow and our initials at either end.

I felt so fraudulent and awful. I know that he means well towards me but we are not right for each other. To be Giancarlo's serious girlfriend would mean catching him between meetings and cities with a perfectly made-up smile, waxed legs and toned skin and that situation would not suit me. Life would be luxurious and comfortable but it would not be a passionate relationship because he doesn't touch my soul. No I'm not in love, and it's impossible to keep up the pretence and so I'll have to move out of his flat.

Beatrice and I had dinner and she asked me if I found him at all attractive. I replied, 'No, not really, but the power of his love and concern and the fact that he can bail me out financially can be intoxicating when there is no one else around who really cares. It seems scary to throw it all away.'

'That's ridiculous,' she scoffed. 'There are many people who care about you. Me, for one.'

'Who else?' I asked, enjoying my self-pity.

'Get a grip,' she said. 'Sapphire, Matthew, Tricky, that guy, Greg, your Aunt May.'

'I'm going to have to move out,' I said to her, 'and I don't know where to go.'

'We'll find something,' she said, 'don't worry.'

September 8th

When Giancarlo telephoned to say he was coming to see me for the weekend, three days after we had slept together, I knew I really had to say something and move out of his flat. I told him I was leaving because I needed some time on my own to think. He tried desperately to persuade me not to go and the next day he telephoned four or five times but the more he tried to impose his will on me, the more suffocated and determined to leave I felt.

A few days earlier Greg had asked me if I would be able to feed his cat while he was away in Greece and I'd said I would. I telephoned Greg and asked him if I could move into his spare room and then we struck a deal. I'm actually sleeping on a sofa bed which has a thin, bumpy mattress, in a room that has no curtains, but at least I've moved out and I'm paying a small rent. Greg isn't around much and when he is he's either on the telephone, or in the bath or watching American football or doing all three at once.

George the cat lies on top of the kitchen door most of the day and makes short bored exits on to the window sill. Not like Tipsy who lived outside – hunting, shooting and fishing, returning when it suited him. I loved it when Tipsy was home because after he'd eaten he would sit on my lap and purr. George twists and catapults out of my arms.

I've written Giancarlo a long letter, trying to explain a few things. I said I was really grateful and appreciative of his hospitality and generosity, but that I didn't think it was a good idea for us to be romantically involved.

Greg has put me in touch with someone who has been hired to find extras for a film being shot next week. I don't want to run out of money again, so I telephoned the woman and she said I could work for two or three days, earning £80 per day, which will pay the rent for three or four weeks. At least this time I know I am hired as an extra and not as an actress with a small part.

September 12th

It's Monday morning and I'm writing in the conservatory at Waterford House. Sapphire, Big John, Greg and I set off to Skara Brae's wedding on Saturday morning in a BMW that Greg had rented. He hadn't been invited to Skara's wedding, but he had asked himself for the weekend at May's and I could hardly refuse.

The wedding was quite moving. I wondered if I would ever get married. It seems so unlikely, because the kind of men I am interested in are not the marrying kind. 'For better or worse, but never for lunch,' is what my father always says, meaning if you want a marriage to work you have to keep a huge amount of space between you, not that marriage has worked for him, distance or no distance.

After the service, there was a lunch-time reception

in the flower-fest marquee. There was kissing, and champagne, and congratulations, and then a drunken toast and a sentimental speech, given by Skara's father. At one moment I thought I saw Doug and my stomach dived and whirled around but when I got nearer, the man was in fact a short blonde woman of about fifty.

We went back to Waterstone in the afternoon. May was out somewhere and the professor was playing chess with himself. We sat around watching television and drinking tea and then went back to the marquee for a large party.

There were 400 people for a sit-down dinner. I was put at the end of a table next to Greg and a small sniffy boy. Suddenly towards the end of the poussin course there was an explosion, a huge explosion, like a bomb going off and all the food slid down the table. I fell off my chair and the food fell on top of me while all around me people were screaming.

Skara's father stood up bravely and made a short, witty speech. Apparently the marquee was built on a hill and the floor had collapsed. He apologised and said if we wanted more food we would have to grope around on the floor for remains. The party limped on but was never quite the same. All the women looked bedraggled: some had ripped buttons and broken shoes, others had stained dresses. The chit-chat was speculative – would Skara's father sue the party-organising company who had put up the marquee and, if so, how much money would he make? More, some people suggested, than he had spent on the party.

And then Greg sidled up to me and with a rattish,

cheeky grin said, 'Has anyone telephoned the papers?' I smiled but then a horrifying thought leapt at me. It must have been Greg who alerted the press about Roberto. That's obviously part of his business, tipping off the papers and receiving hand-outs for his trouble. It all made perfect sense. I confronted him and he blushed and denied it, but he had given himself away. 'How could you?' I said. 'How could you do something like that? How could you go through with a sympathy charade, rushing over to comfort me with a box of éclairs?' I didn't give him a chance to say anything else. I wanted to get away from him. I rushed up to Big J and Sapphire and said, 'No questions. Greg won't be coming with us, we'll have to telephone for a cab.'

So here I am. I have to get back to London to do the film extra work, but I obviously won't be staying at Greg's. Sapphire and Big J went back to London last night, but I stayed here, unsure of exactly where to go. May said I could stay in her London flat, but I know she wouldn't really feel comfortable if I was there for more than one night. I wouldn't either. Her flat has a lingering fusty smell, and it's furnished with antiques, fragile chandeliers and faded silk lampshades.

September 13th

I'm at Stella's. I haven't really seen her yet, because I left the house at six to get to the film set. Greg haunts me, how could anyone be so insidious? I thought he was a friend, but really he's a devious little rat.

The shoot was at Luton Hoo, a house near Milton Keynes. Funnily enough I had been recruited to be an extra in a wedding scene, instructed to appear dressed as if I was going to a wedding. I had borrowed a beautiful, pink, velvet Bella Freud suit from Tricky, who is a stylist, but the wardrobe woman wouldn't let me wear it. She said that pink didn't go with the colour scheme of the scene. Instead she gave me a checked navy blue and red nylon suit from a High Street chain store. It smelt of old sweat and I felt awful in it.

The cameras were set up in a huge room with tables set for a sit-down lunch at a wedding reception. I was allocated to a table and sat down to find Nick the boy from the acting school audition sitting there. 'God,' I said, laughing with relief.

'Babe,' he said, 'we were destined to meet again.'

At the break we went outside to the grounds and smoked a joint. 'How's everything?' I asked.

'Broke,' he said, 'broke, but fairly happy. I've got myself an agent but there's not much work around, that's why I'm here today.'

We talked for a while and he said he'd like to be in touch with me. 'I'm staying with my mother at the moment, but I need somewhere to live, if you hear of anything . . .'

'Well, if you need to crash, call me,' he said, writing his number down on the empty packet of Rizlas. 'It's good to see you,' he said, 'it really is.'

September 16th

I finished filming with £240 in my pocket. Stella is really down, because Dad has gone off to Nassau with his PA, ostensibly to look for premises to set up an office there. She says he makes her feel crazy and that she doesn't believe anything he says anymore. Tonight we had a huge, near fatal, row because she asked me to go to Nassau to spy on him.

I didn't know if she was joking or not, but I said, 'Don't be ridiculous, of course I couldn't do that.' She then accused me of being disloyal and we had a huge fight. 'You've never once said you love me,' I shouted hysterically, 'not once in my whole life. Why should I do anything for you?'

'It's not something I have said to anyone,' she said. 'But I must love you or I wouldn't have put up with all this for so long.' She opened her arms as if to say she wouldn't have put up with the kitchen in such an alarming state of disarray.

'You have never been there for me when I need you,' I said. 'When I need you you are never there for me.'

'So why do you keep trying?' she said. 'Why do you keep asking for my help?'

That froze me up. I left the room quite calmly and found the Rizla packet with Nick's number on it. I called him and asked him if I could move in right away.

Just before I left Giancarlo telephoned. I have no idea how he knew I was there because I hadn't spoken to him since I moved out, but actually it was a relief to hear his voice. I was in an hysterical state and sobbed down the telephone. 'Darling,' he said, which made me cry more, 'darling, why don't you go back to my flat?'

'I can't, Giancarlo,' I said, 'I can't, it would be wrong.'

'If you get into trouble,' he said, 'you must promise to call me.'
Nick's house is filthy.

September 18th

Nick hadn't told me that there was only one bed, which we have been sharing. Last night we drank a large amount of American whiskey and he gave me a couple of yellow egg-shaped pills which he calls jellies and swallows like sweeties, belying the fact that they are prescriptive sleeping pills. After the cocktail of drink and pills, I fell into a loose and hazy state, and we ended up sleeping together.

He's a wonderful lover, but the morning, this morning, was seedy. He has a phobia about light and doesn't like a crack to filter through the window. When we woke up it was nearly 1.00 p.m. The bathroom is revolting, really filthy, and is almost beyond the point of no return, particularly the large, dark brown stain in the loo. The kitchen floor is slippery with grime and the sink is overbrimming with dirty pots and dishes.

September 20th

Nick didn't get up at all yesterday. I telephoned Dad in Nassau last night, collect, because I felt lost and desperate.

'How are you?' he asked. I burst into tears. 'What is it, darling?'

'Everything. When are you coming back?'

'I'm staying here for a while, setting up the business.'

'With your PA?'

'No, she's left. I'm looking for someone else.'

'I'll do it,' I said, 'whatever it is.'

'Can you type?'

'Yes.' I can half type. I started a teach yourself course, when I lived in Dorset. 'Please, Dad, you don't know what's going on, I have nowhere to live, I hate Stella, I'm broke.'

'Come on then,' he said. 'Give it a try, for a while. I'll buy you the ticket, but I obviously won't be paying full PA rates.'

'Can I come tomorrow?' I asked.

September 21st

Nick and I went out last night, very late, to an Egyptian restaurant in Queensway. Dark, black-eyed dancers jellied their bellies, while Egyptian business men smoked tobacco through long, curling hokey-pipes. Nick and I asked for a pipe and they put a large lump of hash in it – soon the place stank of hashish. The manager dealt with us in a very cool manner. He took away the pipe, saying he wanted to clean it and brought it back having disposed of our small brown lump.

We discussed ourselves and decided it would be better to be friends than lovers. Nick already has a French model in Paris anyway. He then gave me a couple of jellies and we drank a bottle of wine and then went home and made love. He woke me early this morning in a state of great excitement because his agent had telephoned and told him to get to an audition for a Levi's ad. He put on a white T-shirt and a pair of black jeans and shaved with an electric shaver and then he drove me to Sapphire's, where I am going to stay for a while on a once-yellow sofa covered in old dog hairs.

I've left a message for Dad to call me.

Dad has just telephoned. He says there is not much

point me coming to Nassau because he had a very bad meeting today and it doesn't look as though he can get the lease he needs on the office building. He says he's returning in about three days, but he's going back to live in his office. 'If you can type,' he said, helpfully, 'why don't you get a temping job?'

September 23rd

Sapphire has won a £500 poetry prize from one of the literary papers.

> Lift me up
> by fingernails
> softly pressing
> the gentle murmur
> of incantation
> scarlet breath on
> my neck. Kiss me
> sweetness there.
>
> Two ladies pass
> unspoken of for years
> sucking their tongues
> closely to teeth, pulling
> their wool around freezing
> bones, clucking in high
> strapped shoes.
>
> I am up. They pass
> catching glances smearing
> licking looks; I arch
> my neck just so
> the softly blank skin
> kissed.

We are all cheered up a great deal by this news and we are going to go out and celebrate tonight.

September 24th

Nick telephoned last night just before we left: he was also in a celebratory mood, because he's been given the part in the Levi's ad. We met at Green Street. Nick was looking dapper and obviously in an elated mood. He had a gramme of coke and so we spent a great deal of time in the ladies, sniffing lines off the top of the loo. I watched him tip the white powder out, place a ten-pound note on top of it and then wipe a credit card up and down over the cash grinding the powder underneath until it was smooth. He then divided the flattened powder into long, thin lines, which we snorted up through the note which he had rolled into a tube. When the club closed at one, we went back to Sapphire's where we all sat, wired and frenzied, talking inanely and making endless cups of tea. We left at 8.00 a.m. and had breakfast at a Portuguese café in the Golborne Road, then Nick did a few errands and we went to bed at about eleven.

I feel blue today. Too many late nights and drugs.

September 25th

Giancarlo tracked me down to Sapphire's. He's coming to London quite soon for a meeting and he wants to see me. He said I sounded very depressed and I agreed that maybe I was and we arranged to have lunch.

Big J is a big slob. He's a painter and decorator, but seems to do very little at Sapphire's, mostly drinking cans of lager and reading tabloids. His lethargy kicked me into action and I got myself off my ass and walked into a temping agency, dressed in an extraordinary brown tweed skirt that I found on the floor of Sapphire's cupboard. I lied like crazy and the woman signed me up.

September 30th

For the last four days I've been working for a PR company, at the reception desk, because the permanent girl had flu. It was an extraordinary set-up – a family firm, and they all call each other by animal names. The son is called Pig! The mother is called Rabbit and the father Badger. Pig is ugly as sin, but sweet and eager to please. They were all very kind to me, particularly Pig and although my tasks were rather dull, I was sad to go.

Today was a disaster. The agency rang first thing this morning and asked me if I could use a XYZ43 switchboard or something like that, so I said yes, as cheerily and heartily as I could. I was sent off to an advertising agency and told to sit at the reception desk and operate the complicated switchboard that flashed and bleeped every few seconds. It was awful. I cut off nearly every call and finally, at about two a woman called me in and said I could go home.

October 2nd

A rushed lunch with GC. He told me I looked tired and pale, which irritated me. 'Have you been taking drugs?' he asked.

'No,' I said. 'Why?'

'You have dark rings under the eyes,' he said. He asked me what I was doing for money and I told him I still have a bit left over from LA, and that I'd signed up with a temping agency but that my last job hadn't gone that well. 'Anna,' he said, 'what is happening in your life?'

'I don't know,' I said. He took my hand.

'I love you. You are very brave. Why don't we get married?'

'Giancarlo!'

'What?' I sat there and thought, he really does love me, maybe I would grow to love him. Maybe if I was financially secure I would be able to get my life together. Maybe sex isn't that important, maybe . . . he would learn . . .

'I can't marry you,' I said finally. 'Really, it wouldn't be right.'

'I understand,' he said, 'but you must go back to my apartment. You cannot go on living like this.'

'Thank you,' I said, weakening, thinking of the dog-haired sofa and Big J's empty lager cans.

October 3rd

Maria was pleased to see me. For twenty-four hours she made me cups of tea and brought me plates of warm, Spanish tortilla. Things are back to normal now, she's lurking around with very little on, listening to jungle music in her bedroom and she's had her nose pierced.

Giancarlo sent me a fax yesterday, asking me to go to a preview of a film by a young Italian director, whom he met on an aeroplane. He is considering investing in his next project and he wants my opinion on his work.

The preview was in Wardour Street. When I arrived, my heart pumped in overdrive because out of the corner of my eye I saw first Doug and then Greg. I walked blinkered towards the bar. Greg came bounding up to me, 'Hi.'

'Hello,' I said coldly, lighting a cigarette.

'This is Karen,' he said, introducing me to a tall black girl.

'Hi,' I said, moving my cigarette into my left hand and putting my drink on to a table. I shook her hand and then picked up the cigarette and drink and went into the cinema, sinking into one of the comfortable armchairs, next to a balding man with a pony tail, carefully placing my coat and bag on the seat next to me.

Greg snivelled to my side and said he had written me a letter but hadn't known where to send it. 'Don't bother,' I said, smiling sweetly. 'Let's forget it.' I meant let's forget that we ever knew each other.

'See you later,' he said, smiling widely and backing away.

Doug was standing in the aisle with another man. I looked down at my *Evening Standard*, and read the first line of my horoscope: *Now is the time to make a break from the past* ... He tapped me on the shoulder. I jumped and turned around and said, 'Oh, *hi*,' sounding surprised as if I hadn't had any idea that he was there.

'Let's have a drink afterwards,' he said, his cruel mouth twisting into a smile.

I couldn't concentrate on the film. I could almost feel Doug's breath behind me. As the credits rolled everybody clapped and my heart started pumping again. I fussed around getting my things together, not wanting to appear too keen to go with him.

'Coming?' he asked me, looking so desirable.

'Yeh, OK,' I said.

The other man smiled at me, shook my hand and walked with us across Wardour Street. Please leave, I willed him away. My wish was granted when he flagged down a cab. So it was just Doug and I walking into Dean Street together. Doug and I. He pulled me towards him and kissed me.

We slipped into the Groucho Club and sat down. He ordered me a glass of champagne and fresh orange juice for himself. We were sitting very close together in the corner of the dining room at a table meant for six. Being with him made me feel heady and I forgot all about the horoscope and his treachery with Eloise. I chain-smoked four cigarettes and drank two more glasses of champagne before standing up to go to the loo.

Nick was standing in reception with a very beautiful girl, who wore her peroxide-coloured hair in two plaits, he introduced her as Françoise, so I presumed she was the French model girlfriend. She was waiting for her French, fur-cuffed coat. I kissed Nick on the lips to show the girl that a little bit of him belongs to me. She went to make a telephone call and Nick and I stood chatting for a while before Doug swung through the doors. Nick kissed me goodbye and grabbed the girl's hand and disappeared through the revolving exit doors.

'Who was that?' Doug asked.

'A friend.'

'He's more than a friend.'

'Is he? Heard from Eloise?' I asked, following him back into the bar.

'No,' he said, 'and I don't suspect I will again.'

'What about all your other lovers?'

'What do you mean?' he smiled.

'You once told me that a man has many lovers, unless it is the real thing.'

'You are the real thing, lovely,' he said.

'We'll see about that,' I said, making a resolution not to sleep with him that night.

He left a message this morning. I haven't called him back. I don't need to. Meaning I know he will call again.

October 5th

Doug came to see me last night. He said he wanted us to go away together. 'Where?' I asked.

'France,' he said. He stayed for a short time, yawned theatrically and then said he was tired and had to go. I wanted to beg him to stay, but I didn't.

After he'd gone, I telephoned Nick because he had left a message. 'So that was the French model,' I said.

'Yes, but she has a name. Françoise.'

'Françoise the French model.'

'French-Canadian. What about blond and handsome?' he asked.

'What about him?'

'Well who was that?'

'That was Doug,' I said, 'the one who nearly broke my heart.'

October 7th

Doug and I went to an exhibition opening of three young conceptual artists at the Saatchi Gallery last night. It felt sexy to be with him and we look good together. One artist had an exhibit of tadpoles swimming inside a giant pair of Perspex platform shoes, which was called 'Down at Heel', and his other exhibit was of mosquitoes buzzing around rows of test-tubes filled with different types of blood inside a large perspex box, entitled, 'That time of the Month'. It was ugly and riveting and rather effective, but I wasn't quite sure what either of them was *really* saying. Maybe that isn't the point. Doug and I went out for dinner and then he drove me home and stayed the night. It was wonderful to be in bed with him again, wonderful and heavenly and sexy-sublime.

Giancarlo telephoned late last night, when Doug and I were in bed. He asked me about the film, and I said I would get back to him. I hadn't really been able to concentrate on the film because of Doug sitting behind me, but it seemed to be about a serial killer. It's one of those manipulative 'splatter' movies that make you laugh, guiltily, as grannies are being raped and dogs are being hurled off roof-tops. Doug knows the director and likes him so we decided to write a glowing report to GC.

October 9th

I am so disappointed. Douglas can't go to France. An advertising agency have asked to see his work, because they are looking for someone to write a series of beer ads. If he gets the job he will earn a huge amount of money. He's preparing for meetings next week and won't talk or think about anything else. He's going to work all weekend. Sapphire, Big J and I are going to a party in Suffolk. I can tell that Sapphire thinks I'm crazy to see Doug again. She hasn't exactly said anything, but her silence on the subject says it all.

October 20th

I'm lying here in the Middlesex Hospital, leg in traction, bored out of my mind. Bloody Big J crashed the car at four in the morning on the way home from the party. I was hunched in the back with Sapphire and I woke lying on the road. I remember moaning and crying out. There was a crowd staring down at me, crazed expressions of concern mixed with gloat-like horror on their faces.

Big J had been speeding through the suburbs at 80mph and apparently went hurtling through a stop sign. A mini-cab came from the left and crashed into my side of the car. The impact of my knee knocking into the seat in front broke my femur – the biggest bone in the body. Sapphire is OK, but bruised her ribs and was in quite a lot of pain. Big J cut his face and the boy who was sitting in the front has a collapsed lung.

Sapphire was horrified by the situation and has split with Big J. He can't understand why she doesn't want to be with him, he thinks it's a momentary lapse caused by shock. Sapphire has been to see me every day, bringing magazines, books, fruit and newspapers. Big J came in once and stood sheepishly at the end of the bed, mumbling apologies. I almost felt sorry for him. He's going to lose his licence as he was well over the limit.

On the night of the crash, at five in the morning, I had a pin inserted under my knee so the leg could be put in traction. The pain was excruciating and I begged the young Asian doctor for a painkiller, but he was adamant that I was to be given nothing, because I was concussed. It was like a scene from *Marathon Man*. The doctor literally *drilled* two holes under the knee and I screamed and cried and begged him not to, but he drilled on anyway, despite my hysteria.

After the drilling I was moved to a ward. My leg was aching and covered in grit and blood. I was crying and wondering what had happened to Sapphire and if anybody knew what was happening to me. 'Never mind,' said a large West Indian woman who was eating a banana in the bed next to mine, 'pray to the Lord and everything will be arlright.' Lord, I asked in my head, why me? Lord, if you get me out of here, I promise to go regularly to church.

I can lie down or sit up. Every night a nurse gives me a couple of sleeping pills because it is impossible to sleep with a leg in traction. I can't go to the loo, have a shower, or wash my hair. The nurses bring me bed-pans and wash me. The food is disgusting.

October 22nd

Darling Doug came in last night. He's freaked by the situation, I can tell. When he saw me for the first time he said: 'God, it's so real.' Doug looks at the world as though looking through a prism, everything has to be

102

fragmented and dissected and then put back together in his own way. He doesn't like hard, defined edges. He's wary of too much pain or too many feelings and he shies away from anything that is out of his control.

The sight of me strung up is too extreme for him. The expression in his eyes has hardened. He's very sensitive and I think he's picked up the vibe that I blame him slightly, but irrationally, for the crash. If we had gone to Paris as planned, I would not have been returning from a party with Big J. He looks uncomfortable when he's here and I feel so unattractive. I should tell him not to visit for a while, but I couldn't bear not to see him. His pride would keep him away for ever. Last night he showed me a book he wants to adapt for a film, the diary of a Victorian maidservant. Then he left, saying he had to go and finish some writing. 'Will you ring me later?' I asked, regretting my tone, which at best was a vulnerable plea and at worst a challenging whine.

'I'll try to,' he said. Then I knew he wouldn't.

October 25th

Mr Norreys is my consultant. He's a bone specialist, and he looks like a man in a forties *Picture Post* illustration of the happy family around the hearth. Mother smiling, pouring tea, daughter playing with a cat, son reading a book and Dad, with Brylcreemed hair, smoking a pipe and listening to the wireless. Mr Norreys is relentlessly cheery, but he reminds me of a minister, cheery against all the odds, exhausted by the

103

crumbling system, harried by too much to do. Tired but never emotional.

Dad has been in a few times. He says his GP told him that Norreys is the best bone man in London. I haven't seen Stella since the second morning. She came in all sweet and maternal, but then something snapped, maybe she caught sight of herself in the mirror. 'You've caused me so much worry,' she said, 'I've aged ten years since your crash.'

I sighed, 'I'm really tired.'

'So am I,' she said. 'I've stopped taking Prozac. It was no longer working for me. I am considering suing Eli Lilly.'

'A lily?'

'Eli . . . Lilly,' she said, accentuating the words in an irritating way. 'The Prozac company. You know, the Prozac company. Made millions out of people like me.'

'No, I don't know it,' I said.

Dad is back from Nassau and still living in his office. The problem is that Stella will not let go, she won't accept that it is over between them. Sometimes I feel sorry for her and understand that she is going through a hard time and that she had a difficult childhood. Her father, like mine, drank too much and died of a liver haemorrhage when she was twelve. Her mother went into a deep decline, and was clinically depressed for three years, ignoring her three daughters.

Rose, the West Indian woman, went home today. Her daughter and three small grandsons came to collect her. She hugged her daughter and grandchildren and wiped away a few tears. I envied their love for

104

each other. It seemed so uncomplicated. She left me some fruit and a card. Now she's had her hip replacement operation she's going back to Barbados for a well-deserved retirement. She has been an office cleaner for the last twenty-five years, earning at best only £4.20 an hour.

After she left I began to cry, thinking I was experiencing some kind of empathy for her hard life. That was true to a certain extent but Rose leaving triggered off emotions swelling inside about Doug abandoning me. Doug not being here for me. Doug. He's breaking my heart.

October 27th

A van-load of beautiful white lilies arrived. My heart sank when I read the card – Love Giancarlo. The nurses oohed and ahed. Nobody had ever seen anything like it. I sent some to the geriatric ward and I wanted to send a tank-load to Rose, but no one knew her address. GC is arriving tomorrow to see me.

Doug breezed in at about eight. He was on his way to a dinner party. He was in such a rush that I became paranoid that he had a girl waiting for him in the car. He gave me a silver ring and kissed me, saying he couldn't stay. I somehow knew that the ring was a goodbye present, a way of absolving his guilt. 'Will you visit tomorrow?'

'It's a busy time, sweetie,' he said, 'but I'll try.'

Do you love me? I wanted to ask, but stopped myself. After he left, I thought how ironic life is. Here I am surrounded by lilies sent by a man I do not love. I'm desperate for Doug but there is nothing I can do. I can't get to him. I can't sleep, worrying about whether he has a girl in his bed or not. He's sure to. He left a scarf here, a beautiful dark brown cashmere scarf. It smells of him and is some comfort.

October 28th

GC arrived straight from the airport with a bag full of duty free bottles of champagne. His first remark after kissing me was, 'My God, you must move to a private room. When you move Carlos can come in and do it up.'

'What are you talking about? Do it up? I'll be out soon.'

'Well, you must have your own room,' he said.

'Giancarlo, I'm fine,' I said, although since Rose has left I've been longing for some privacy. A woman who never stops talking to herself, even when she is asleep, has moved into the empty bed.

October 30th

I've moved into a palatial private room. I have my own television and telephone. The nurses have time to chat. The sister is a permed-hair male named Phil who doesn't seem to like me. Despite my protests, Giancarlo's decorator, Carlos arrived this afternoon with a rug, some vases, a few cushions and a tapestry wall-hanging. Sister Phil looked horrified. This afternoon he persecuted me with a foul-textured medicine which is meant to make my bowels move.

106

What a life. I think Nick is coming in tonight. God I hope so.

October 31st

Nick came in last night. We smoked a joint and I talked about Doug. I'm desperate because he's taken off to the country to write the beer ads. We've only spoken once briefly in the last two days. Nick says I should relax and everything will be fine, but I intuitively know it's all over. We watched *Blind Date* on television and laughed at a row of male triplets. Nick asked for some sleeping pills, but I explained that I was only given two a night. 'I've got to have some,' he said. 'I haven't been able to sleep for four days.' I asked Helen, my favourite nurse. At first she was reluctant, but we managed to persuade her, although she said it was the first and last time.

November 5th

Giancarlo came to say goodbye yesterday afternoon. He was very sweet and brought me some food from Luigi's deli on the Fulham Road. He stroked my forehead before he left and said, '*Povera bambina.*' I surprised myself and asked him not to go. He makes me feel safe. He said he would be back soon.

It's hell waking up so early every morning, particularly because there is nothing to look forward to. Mr Norreys usually comes in at about 7.15 a.m. Tomorrow morning he's going to examine my leg under general anaesthetic. Apparently in ninety-nine per cent of cases, the bone fuses together naturally. I've been here for nearly a month, so the bone should really be gelling.

Douglas telephoned last night. He's finished the first draft of the script and today he's going to Paris to see some friends. I asked him when he'd be back and he said at the end of the week. He gave me his telephone number, but I sensed he was irritated that I had asked. He said he prefers to communicate by fax.

Everyone but me seems to have a life. Throwing firework parties no doubt, loving couples sharing a sparkler.

November 7th

Yesterday was hell. I woke up from the anaesthetic feeling weepy to find May sitting by my bed. 'Poor, poor darling,' she said, kissing me dramatically twice on each cheek. 'Now, you know I hate hospitals so I won't stay for long. I'm meeting Alice, Lee and Anthea for a session of bridge.'

She had brought a home-made hamper – two bottles of red wine, a bottle of elderflower cordial, a pot of lavender honey, a huge box of chocolates from Rococo that I had given her for Christmas last year and some rice crackers.

Mr Norreys says the bone hasn't moved very much. I'll have to stay in hospital for God knows how much longer. I couldn't be more depressed. When GC telephoned and I told him the news he said he would be back next week to see me.

108

I telephoned Doug late last night. His friend answered and said he had gone to the country to visit somebody, and would be back tomorrow. I was embarrassed to telephone so late and then paranoid that maybe he was visiting a lover.

November 8th

Haven't heard from Doug.

November 9th

I telephoned Doug last night. He said he had just walked in, which was dire. We spoke for a few minutes and then he asked if he could telephone me back. I waited edgily all night, but he never did call.

Sapphire washed my hair for me today. She's found an agent who thinks she may be able to find her a publisher.

November 11th

Doug telephoned yesterday afternoon and said he was still in Paris and would be staying there all week. After the call, I felt better for a while, but I then became convinced that he was not really in Paris at all. I dialled 1471 which gives the last number dialled, and I was right, it gave his London number.

I lay brooding for an hour and then telephoned his London number and left a message on his answering machine, saying I had a strange feeling he was in town.

I was feeling despondent, when Giancarlo telephoned. He said he couldn't make it over for another ten days. 'Why not?' I asked, suddenly really wanting him to be here to stroke my forehead and hold my hand. He told me all about some urgent business affairs, but I wasn't listening. I am finding it more and more difficult to concentrate on anything.

November 12th

It's late. I've become immune to sleeping pills and sleep fitfully, waking three or four times every night. The Doug affair is preying on my mind, but he hasn't been in touch.

The last thing I needed was a visit from Greg. He arrived this evening with a large bunch of flowers. 'Can't stop,' he said to my relief, 'just thought I would see how you were doing.' As he was leaving Dad walked in with a package wrapped in silver foil. 'Hello,' said Greg, shaking Dad's hand, 'Greg Cohen.'

'Hello,' Dad said. 'Would you like to stay for a bit of cold salmon? Anna, let's get some service.'

'I don't know, Dad. The smell is so *fishy*, it's making me feel sick.'

'Of course it's fishy, silly girl. It's salmon.' Dad went to the door and spoke to Phil in the corridor. A few minutes later Phil entered, groaning and sighing, bearing plates and cutlery.

Greg and Dad completely ignored me. Greg was

110

boasting to Dad about how much experience he has in the restaurant business. My heart plummeted when Greg suggested they open one together. I turned the television on. Phil walked in with my supper and Dad absent-mindedly asked him for some ground pepper, a napkin and the bill.

It was a nightmare. They left together, so I had no chance to warn Dad off Greg: I tried to telephone him at home, but there was no reply.

November 21st

Postcard from Douglas sent from Paris, four days ago. He said nothing about my message on his machine. He's staying in Paris until January. I have no more energy to get worked up or to cry.

November 22nd

Last night I drank half a small bottle of neat vodka that Nick left here last time he visited and then I watched myself dial the number and heard the slow, French ringing tone. It was my voice asking for Doug, and then after a long wait, I heard his footsteps approaching and he said, 'I don't want any scenes.' Later in the conversation, I accused him of lying when he last telephoned me. He said he was sorry and that he had lied because he felt confused. He said all sorts of rubbish, including something about needing to be in Paris. And then he said he would call me tomorrow.

'Will you?' I asked.

'Yes,' he said. It's the worst torture of all. Why

111

do I put myself through it?

November 24th

I am highly embarrassed and fraught. Nick came in here last night, slightly drunk. I had asked him to come and see me because I was so upset about Doug not telephoning when he said he would. He had brought a bottle of champagne which we drank. He asked about Doug and I told him the pitiful tale. 'Leave it,' he said. 'Leave him alone. He's a psycho case.' He hugged me and then we were kissing.

'Darling,' he said, kissing me again. 'I don't want to think of you with him.' It was very sexy, he's a good, passionate kisser. He lay next to me on the bed and then he was on top of me, contorted around my leg in traction and we were fucking. A few minutes later a nurse walked in, which goes down as the most embarrassing moment of my life. He managed to get off me, quickly, but there wasn't enough time to pull his trousers up. He climbed into bed next to me, his trousers around his ankles.

'Get out of that bed,' the nurse said.

'I can't,' he said. 'I can't.'

'Out now.'

'I can't.'

'Right,' she said, 'I'll be back in a minute.' Nick climbed out and was pulling up his trousers when Phil marched in and my face heated up again, although it was hard not to giggle. When Mr Norreys arrived this morning he said that from now on no one would be allowed to sit on my bed. He didn't actually say why, but it was perfectly obvious that he knew everything.

112

He also said they were going to put me out again tomorrow to check the leg.

I spoke to Dad, but it's not good, he thinks Greg is great and is enmeshed in a deal with him. I think they are going to open a restaurant together.

November 26th

It's late. Very late, and I still feel groggy. When I came round from the anaesthetic darling Giancarlo was in the room. I felt weepy and burst into tears. He gave me a hug and held my hand for a long time. At last he said, 'I have something for you.'

'What?' I asked weakly.

He handed me a small box. Inside was the most beautiful ruby and diamond ring.

'Will you marry me? This is the last time I ask.'

The ring sat there on its puffed white cushion, just waiting to be tried on. I put it on the fourth finger of my left hand and then I smiled and said, 'Thank you.' He kissed me gently on the lips.

'Giancarlo,' I said. 'Get me out of here, please.'

November 28th

Mr Norreys has told me that the bone is not fusing together, so I am that one per cent statistic. Of course I would be. Today Giancarlo sent in a young smart GP. 'I've got to get out of here,' I said to the man, who was good-looking and wearing a pinstripe suit. 'I'm going mad. I can't eat, read, go to the loo. I have lost all sense of concentration.'

'You can have an operation,' he said, 'which

means you would be able to leave in a couple of weeks.'

'I'll do it,' I said. 'Let me do that.'

November 30th

The operation, I have been told, is long and quite complicated and I will lose a massive amount of blood. They are going to graft some bone from my lower back and wrap it around the femur with a metal plate. Giancarlo is going to stay in London for the operation. We're getting married as soon as I am well enough to walk. Countess di Trevi, so *je ne sais quoi*.

December 5th

The pain is harrowing. I am given pethidine injections every three hours in my thigh. Great big wopping injections which soothe the pain but have made my thigh almost numb. I have intravenous drips in my arms, dripping blood. The place where the bone has been taken is particularly agonising. Apparently a bone graft is the most painful operation possible. Stella came in for the first time in weeks. I was too weak to care and could hardly keep my eyes open. She left a box of chocolates. Giancarlo is here heroically, most of the time.

December 12th

I took my first step today with crutches. I felt so weak and feeble and my legs are like sticks. I am

114

thin thin thin. Giancarlo is taking me to Claridge's when I get out.

December 14th

I'm leaving tomorrow. Giancarlo and I gave a party for the nurses. Phil managed a smile. They all congratulated me on my marriage and I thanked them, but when I showed off my ring it seemed to flash in the most ominous, knowing kind of way.

December 16th

We are staying in a suite at Claridge's. The bedroom has an art deco mirror and two deco ceiling lights hanging down like large breasts. Giancarlo and I share a bed. He massages my shoulders, but his hands slip no further because of my fragile leg.

Sapphire, Matthew, Tricky and Beatrice came for tea today. A fresh-faced young man delivered a large silver platter, laden with scones, cream, strawberry jam and fifty sandwiches with the crusts scrupulously sliced off.

Beatrice brought a man called Nev, whom she met last weekend. He's a tall man with square shoulders and unruly hair. He's a graphic designer and quite attractive. It's strange but I heard myself commissioning him to design our wedding invitations.

December 19th

Back at the flat. Giancarlo carried me up the stairs, even though I was perfectly capable of going up with the crutches.

We have set a date for the wedding, 28th January. I telephoned Stella and she sounded pleased for a moment, but then she banged on in a desultory fashion, first about Christmas and then about how she has been putting out crumbs for the birds.

Giancarlo wants me to have my wedding dress designed by Christian Lacroix. Beatrice and I are going to Paris together for an appointment. GC will join us for Christmas.

December 20th

Today I took a cab to 192 and hobbled in with the crutches to meet Nev and discuss wedding invitations. He was doing a crossword and appeared not to notice me standing there.

'Hello,' I said.

'Hi, man.' He looked wired and frenetic. 'Hello,' he said, kissing me. 'What do you want to drink.'

'Champagne, please.'

'Right, fine, no problem,' he said, a touch sarcastically.

He kept asking me if I was in love with GC. I laughed but didn't reply. 'Well, I've done research on him,' he said. 'His business dealings are a little dodgy.'

'Are they?' I said. 'How would you know?'

'That would be telling,' he said.

December 21st

Beatrice and I are on the way to Paris in business class, drinking more champagne. She's just been probing me about what made me accept Giancarlo's proposal.

'Because he loves me,' I said, 'because I'm tired of unreliable men and I'm tired.'

'But do you love him?'

'Yes.'

'But you're not attracted to him,' she said in an accusative tone.

'I am . . . well not passionately.'

'I thought you hated going to bed with him.'

'I never said that,' I said, but the confrontation made me uneasy. I haven't actually had to make love with him since leaving hospital. He doesn't make my heart leap when I look at him, but there is more to life, isn't there? It's not possible to have everything, is it?

Here we are at the Ritz, Ritz, Ritz. Much more glamorous than Claridge's. The bedroom is an outrageous salmon pink affair, with rococo frills and curls and a nude by Renoir above the bed. The view is of a courtyard – greenery and fountains.

Maria obviously told Nev that I was at the Paris Ritz because when we arrived there were already two messages to call him. Urgently. Frankly.

I just called him. 'It's me,' I said. 'Anna.'

'Oh hi. Look, can I call you back.'

'I thought it was urgent.'

'It is.'

I've waited ten minutes but he hasn't called, so we're going out.

December 22nd

Spent the morning limping around a small patch of the Louvre, without the crutches, and the afternoon at Lacroix. There was the inevitable cluster of Japanese tourists paying homage to the 'Mona Lisa'. Snapping. I had never been to the Louvre before, but had imagined that the 'Mona Lisa' would be in a room of its own, hung above a golden plinth, with a red carpet leading up to it or something, but it was hung in a dark corridor.

I was exhausted after the Louvre excursion and my appointment at the Lacroix studios was an intimidating experience. A chic woman in charge of haute couture greeted us and spoke fierce, fast French, although later I heard her speaking perfectly good English on the telephone. My French is not up to understanding fast and fierce conversation, so I nodded and let Beatrice translate. Everything about this woman was elegant, including her fingernails and as she showed me more and more exquisite samples I began to feel deeply and hugely ungainly, particularly because of my limp and my slightly dirty jeans.

A small man measured me, inside arm, outside leg, bust, neck, wrist etc. Lacroix came in for a second, which is unheard of apparently. He looked me up and down, smiled briefly and then spoke to Beatrice in French. 'Would you be willing to leave it to him?' she asked. 'He wants to show off your legs.'

'Does he mind the limp?' I asked. 'Perhaps I shouldn't have a tiny mini.'

'Ze dress, it's for a wedding, *n'est-ce pas?*' he said.

He drew a sketch. It's rather outrageous – it is a mini dress but it has a long trailing back. 'God,' said Beatrice when we got into the street, 'how much do you think it will cost?' I have no idea, although Beatrice guessed about twenty grand, which seems very excessive.

December 25th

GC arrived this morning. We spent the whole day in his suite, eating and drinking. As more and more food and drink went in and out of the door, I began to feel disgustingly pampered, like an idle princess, buffeted around on a mink cushion. Nev's words about Giancarlo's dodgy business dealings were ringing in my ears as I contemplated how he could possibly afford to be quite so extravagant – a suite at the Ritz apparently costing about £4,000 per night. He says part of his Ritz stay is research, because he is opening a glitzy hotel in Italy, somewhere near the sea.

There was a fax delivered to the room, sent from Nev: 'Happy Christmas. Wonder what you are up to. Wish I was there. How many invitations needed?'

Giancarlo gave me an old Cartier watch with our initials entwined on the back. It's very elegant and very beautiful. My present to him of an aquamarine-coloured cashmere scarf that May had given me seemed rather paltry in comparison.

I thought Beatrice seemed a little depressed when she said goodnight, so I asked her if she wanted to stay the night with us in the bed which is as big as a small island. Giancarlo gave me a horrified look, but luckily Beatrice didn't take up the offer. I lay in Giancarlo's arms and he stroked my forehead, then he kissed me and he smelt familiar, of crushed lime, and his kiss was rather soft and sexy and then he stroked my hair again and lulled me luxuriously to sleep.

December 26th

Giancarlo left at lunch time and then Beatrice and I went swimming in the health club downstairs. My physiotherapist said that swimming would be good for my leg, so I swam about seven lengths and heard the underwater music rippling through my ears and thought, life with Giancarlo is really very good, and being too rich to walk and too bored to talk is rather wonderful.

Beatrice gets all angst-ridden in the morning before breakfast. She comes into my room and eats two *pains au chocolat* and hot chocolate and coffee and then she has a cigarette and calms down. Every time we go out she insists on going via a macaroon shop called La Duree. The macaroons are delicious, but I have to grab them when I can because Beatrice always buys a box of twelve and eats them compulsively on the street.

The Renoir is a fake. Beatrice always said it was, but I wanted to believe it was genuine. She rang the manager this morning, first thing, after the first croissant, to check. It was such a disappointment. I wanted to believe that anything was possible at the Paris Ritz, that Renoirs did just hang on the walls.

I keep signing scandalous bills. The Ritz sandwiches which we ordered the first night cost the equivalent of £30. Beatrice is talking about giving a dinner for Giancarlo when she gets back, but I know he wouldn't appreciate the way she uses an old door as a table or her delicious but erratic cooking that is served *à la* Spanish hours, at about midnight. He would freak with the chaos and the disorder, and I

121

can hear him say, 'What are those two rats doing there?' pointing at Beatrice's hamsters, Biggy and Bobo.

December 28th

It had to happen. It was always at the back of my mind. Yesterday we bumped into Doug – twice. First time we were having a coffee in a café called La Palette near the Beaux Arts. I was sitting with Beatrice being stared at by a sexy fuck-me stranger when I saw Doug. There he was, in the corner with a man. My heart was pumping and hurdling. I looked away, looked back and he caught my eye and raised his eyebrow. 'Don't go over,' Beatrice whispered. '*Don't.*' I knew she was right. He waved and smiled and then I said let's get out of here and we left without looking back. In the street, I felt desperate, darkened and confused.

Then later that night we went to a restaurant called Natasha's, owned by a Russian woman called Natasha. She has photographs of herself and various celebrities displayed all over the dark purple walls. We were taken by a friend of Giancarlo's, a sweet boring friend called Edmondo something who works at the Italian embassy. We sat down and twenty minutes later Doug came in with big-lipped Beatrice Dalle. This time he came up and kissed me. 'What's up?' he whispered in my ear. I showed him my engagement ring.

He looked a little thrown which pleased me. Beatrice coughed. 'Beatrice Dalle,' he said. She shook Edmondo's hand and then said, '*J'ai faim,*' and walked away, ignoring Beatrice and me.

'Better go,' Doug said. 'We're talking film projects. I'll call you soon.'

Of course it threw me into a plunging spiral. I couldn't sleep all night and I nearly telephoned him at least ten times. This morning I feel much better because I have finally made the decision that he is a wayward heart-breaker and I can do without him. My heart can't take any more pumping.

December 30th

I'm back in London. Giancarlo telephoned four times this morning. He has some absurdly expensive tickets for a charity New Year's Eve ball at the Metropolitan Museum and he wants me to accompany him. I asked him why they were so expensive, and he said it was because Diana, the peevish princess, is rumoured to be honouring New York society with her presence, supposedly sitting at the same table as John Kennedy.

'You haven't given me enough notice,' I said.

'Surely you plan to spend New Year in New York with me.'

'But Giancarlo,' I said, 'my leg.'

As far as I am concerned, New Year's Eve is the same as any other night, except one has to stay up later and drink a bit more and kiss people one would never normally kiss. Having said that I may go *really* wild on the eve of the millennium. I may kiss a stranger, passionately, as if for the last time.

January 1st

Nev telephoned a few times yesterday and then turned up last night with a couple of friends – a man with a pallid face and thin, long, hair who looked as though he tripped through the sixties and a young girl who wore masses of beads around her neck and a long dress appliquéd with tiny flowers.

'What's happening?' Nev asked as he walked through the door.

'Nothing,' I shrugged.

'Any parties?' the man named Robin asked.

'I really don't know,' I said.

Nev made a few telephone calls while the man from the sixties packed grass into a small pipe with an ivory handle and talked at length about a book called *The Celestine Prophecy* which has been a best-seller in America.

'It's a novel about an ancient manuscript discovered in Peru which illuminates the nine key insights into life,' he said, inhaling deeply on the pipe and passing it on to Nev, before exhaling a thick cloud of smoke. 'The premise of the book is that we're moving towards a completely spiritual culture on earth, man, which I believe we are. Don't you think, Nev?'

'Yeh, that's true, man, very true.' Nev inhaled. 'It's happening now!' he said flinging up his arms. '*NOW.*'

'It's already happened to me,' the girl said, leaning forward to reach the pipe that was being passed to her from Nev. 'I experience a Higher Power every day. I look to my Higher Power before making any important decisions,' she said.

We ended up at a party in West London, although there was some fantastical talk about driving up to Scotland and taking a ferry to the mainland of the Orkney Islands. The pallid man said it would be good to spend the first day of the New Year by the standing stones. 'Far better than Stonehenge,' he said. 'Far-out.'

'Yeh, let's go,' Nev said, wanting to believe we would. 'Let's go.'

We never discovered who was giving the party in West London. It was a party of vaguely recognisable faces, of people standing on the stairs. I followed Nev downwards towards the kitchen. 'Don't mind me,' a boy said, flattening himself against the wall. 'I'm only a painting.'

Nev and I stayed in the kitchen, chatting about nothing in particular. We watched people come and go and remarked on them once they'd left. 'Why don't you cancel the wedding and marry me?' he said. I laughed in a silly, dismissive way as though he had asked me to fly to the moon. 'No I'm serious,' he smiled his particular ironic half-smile. I laughed again. 'What's so funny?'

We left before midnight in a 'unit', as Nev calls it, with Robin and his young, blonde girl. 'I wanted to stay,' the girl, Honey, said. 'I'd like to have seen New Year.'

'You can see it anywhere,' Nev said. 'Come back with us.'

Nev lit a few candles in his room and produced a bottle of Black Label. We toasted each other at midnight and sang a couple of rounds of 'Auld Lang Syne'. Nev had turned the radio on so we heard Big Ben striking midnight. 'To us,' Nev said, looking at me. 'May we live happily ever after.'

January 8th

Twenty days to go until I'm married. *Vogue* have
asked to photograph me, for something about English
girls marrying Europeans, and this morning *Hello*
magazine telephoned and asked if they could photograph our wedding. 'No, I don't think so,' I said,
pausing for a second to see if they would offer
cash.

'Are you sure? It would be very tasteful,' the
girl cajoled, 'a record of your special day.' What
is it worth? I wanted to say, having heard rumours
that *Hello* pay hundreds of thousands of pounds.
But no money was offered. The whole question is
a redundant one anyway because Giancarlo would
never agree. Thank God. I can't quite see myself
staring luridly out of the pages.

Stella won't admit it, but she loves the idea that
I will be a contessa, albeit an Italian one. She telephoned this evening and I told her about *Hello*. 'Oh,
but you should do it,' she said. 'I'd love to send copies
to my friends in America.'

'Why can't you send them photographs?' I asked.

'It's not the same. Everyone has wedding photographs. Not everyone has them printed in a magazine.'

'*Hello* is hardly a magazine,' I said, 'it's more
like a catalogue of who not to invite for dinner.'

Matthew Clivesmith has re-named me La Contessa.

127

'Contessa, darling, it's me,' he says when he telephones. 'Darling,' he said the other day, 'there are too many counts to count in Italy. Maybe you should stay here.'

January 10th

A wonderful two days in Paris. I returned by the Euro-Star train and was shocked. Shocked by how dinky England is. When we left Paris, the sun shone and we sped along at 200mph. But once we emerged from the tunnel it was like going through the looking glass, back in time to Dinkland, circa 1950. The sky was heavy with cloud, and the train slowed down to 30mph because Network South East haven't yet changed the tracks to suit the new train.

We chuffed past dinky sheep, in dinky little fields, before hitting the glum-slum of South London: the power stations, the third world high streets and the nasty little houses that back on to the tracks. The French would never put up with it. At Waterloo we were confronted by boarder control. A plain clothes police man asked me what I'd been doing in Paris.

'Pleasure or business?'

'Having a great deal of pleasure minding my own business,' I replied.

I spent two tantalising days in the Isle St Louis, in Giancarlo's parents' flat. The ceiling has original wooden beams, the drawing room and bedroom look over the Seine. The apartment was empty except for a good-looking man, a butler, Jean-Pierre, who had nothing much to do except look after me. He brought me fruit in the morning, with *pains au chocolat* and a light Madeira cake and thin tea was poured into delicate cups from a heavy silver teapot. He drove me to my fittings and hung around discreetly waiting for me to finish. On the second night, I dialled Doug's number once but there was no reply. Jean-Pierre took me to a club in the rue Bude that night, a small intimate club, and we danced and drank beer and then he walked me home, and went back to the club on his own.

I have a small spot on my chin and tried to cancel the session with *Vogue* tomorrow, but the woman said the make-up artist would be able to conceal any blemishes. Giancarlo's family are very disappointed that the wedding is at Waterford and not in Rome.

January 12th

I arrived at the studio half an hour late. It was packed with people – the photographer, his two assistants, about four women from *Vogue*, the hairdresser, hairdresser's assistant, a girl whose only job appeared to be making tea and organising food and a couple of other people who loitered aimlessly. The make-up man cleaned my face, and plucked my eyebrows, chatting incessantly, something about the February cover of *The Face*.

It was too early in the day for me to react and I haven't seen *The Face*, so I smiled vaguely and flicked through a newspaper, hoping he wouldn't say anything about the spot. The hairdresser then yanked me with a comb, pulled my hair into odd positions, gelled and sprayed me. The assistant's only job was to hand over a couple of pins.

130

One of the *Vogue* girls asked me a few questions about myself and Giancarlo. When she asked me where we were going to live, I said, 'Between Rome, New York and London,' which I immediately regretted because it sounds so spoilt and *Dolce Vita*, so I asked her to change Rome, New York and London to London, but she somehow managed to persuade me that using all three was more pertinent to the theme of the article.

I had imagined that I would be in and out of the studio in an hour, but it took four and I was late for lunch with Dad. Later GC telephoned and asked me where our wedding list was and I had to admit I had no idea. I had completely forgotten that people give presents. 'Thank God I have to remind you,' he said.

'Listen,' I said. 'I'm not marrying myself, there are two of us involved in this.'

January 15th

Nev was meant to deliver our invitations last night, but he telephoned to say they were not quite ready. Giancarlo had a fit and said we would have to postpone the wedding. I think it would cause far too much grief to postpone now. Giancarlo has decided to fly over tomorrow. He's worried that nothing will get done if he's not around.

January 17th

The invitations were sent out yesterday. Giancarlo and I met at Conran to choose the presents. GC wants

131

to rent a cottage in Oxfordshire and he chose practical items to furnish it with, like china and rugs, while I lingered over vast pots of sweets and a beautifully designed, but totally impractical chair. GC became more and more tetchy and impatient, because he had a few meetings scheduled for the afternoon. I was drifting in a dream and in the end it seemed easier to let him choose everything. Afterwards we went to the oyster bar, below Bibendum, but I couldn't seem to make a decision about what I wanted to eat.

'Let me choose for you,' Giancarlo said finally.

'No it's all right. I'll have the smoked salmon and scrambled eggs. No I'll have the crab salad. Actually I'll just have a beer and some soup.' The waiter, who was busy crossing out and rewriting, sighed and turned quickly after my soup decision.

'What is the matter with you?' Giancarlo asked. He had now lost patience and was looking agitated.

'I don't know,' I said, improvising quickly, hoping to win the power back. 'I don't know if I can go through with it.'

'Through with what? The soup?'

'No, the wedding.'

I was expecting him to plead with me, but he called my bluff. He put his napkin down on the table, stood up, and said, 'Fine.' He placed a fifty-pound note under the ashtray and walked towards the door. Of course I ran after him, his reaction made me respect and want him that bit more.

January 20th

Giancarlo has gone back to New York for a few days.

Last night Matthew had a dinner party to celebrate his thirtieth birthday. Nev made an entrance during coffee and pulled up a chair next to me. Matthew gave him a drink and made a small-talk remark about how much he was looking forward to my wedding.
'If she goes through with it,' Nev said.
I laughed. 'Well, it's true, you may marry me instead.' I looked at him and thought perhaps, just maybe. Despite his mothy appearance he has a wonderful sense of humour and he is so talented, unique and perverse.
But after dinner, we went back to the one room, for one last drink and of course we drank more than one and I left at dawn and thought, no, I cannot live my life like this.

January 21st

I took the train to Stroud and May met me at the station. She's chosen 'Trumpet Tune' by Purcell for my entrance to the church and the 'Gloria' by Vivaldi for the exit. Sapphire is going to read the 'Bridal Song' by Shakespeare and I want someone to read the *Song of Solomon*, chapter 7, verses 6 and 7. There are twelve guests staying for the wedding including GC's parents. My nerves are parachuting. I have secretly hired Nev to take wedding photographs.

January 22nd

Back in London. Presents have started to arrive. I've already opened four ashtrays with elephants painted on them and a Venetian coloured-glass chandelier plus a few boxes of kitchen equipment. We have decided not to have any speeches. Giancarlo is not particularly witty and his best man apparently doesn't speak very good English. Dad should make a slurred speech, but frankly I'd rather he didn't.

GC is having his stag party tonight. He's invited my father, three friends from Harvard Business School, his two brothers and an ex-girlfriend from Rome. They are having dinner at The Ivy. GC asked me if I wanted to join him after dinner, but I declined, feigning tiredness, but the truth is that I am going to meet Nev for a drink.

January 23rd

GC's brothers, his friends from Harvard Business School and our respective parents met last night for a strenuous drink. Stella laughed intermittently, high-pitched laughter that sliced through the room. Dad arrived very late and then chatted up GC's mother, while Stella looked on furiously. GC's father took me by the hand and said how happy he was that I was marrying his son and how much he and his wife were looking forward to having grandchildren. Grandchildren, the idea, my hands began to sweat and the room was closing in.

It was so liberating to meet Nev later. We drank tequilas, three or four each, and then I began to feel spacy and strange, seeing the world as if from a great height. We laughed about the wedding and Nev promised that when the priest asks is there any reason why these two should not be joined in holy matrimony, or whatever it is he asks, he would put up his hand and think of a good reason.

We stayed up all night. Nev was drawing me: I lay on his bed and he drew me for four or five hours. We stopped for cigarette breaks and he massaged my shoulders. His hands are strong, and when he massaged me I felt frail and feminine and I wanted him to crush me. Today I am shattered and write this in bed. I am guilt- and angst-ridden about not getting up and facing the day.

January 26th

I'm resting in Gloucestershire. Hungover. Last night Beatrice, Sapphire, Tricky and I went out to celebrate my last few days of freedom. We drank cranberry and vodka at Beatrice's and then we went to a party given by Bellanna's ex-boyfriend, Rock. The party was dreadful, everyone dressed in black and too trendy and bored to talk.

We left and hailed a cab, not knowing where we were going. In the end we went back to the flat and lay about on the sofa, giggling. Giancarlo came in wearing a dressing-gown, and gave me a tired impatient look and said, 'Anna, perhaps you may be over-doing things. You should come to bed and rest your leg.' Bed was the last thing on my mind, particularly with him and my leg was actually feeling fine, so I nodded and smiled until he left the room.

'Oh my God, the reading,' I said, 'I haven't got anyone to read the *Song of Solomon*.'

Tricky suggested Matthew Clivesmith and then telephoned and woke him up. We took the telephone in turn and persuaded and cajoled him to come over: darling, we said endlessly, we are *desperate* to see you, quite frankly it's a matter of life and death.

'You'll have to pay for my cab,' he sighed at last with the tone of an indulged lover, who was enjoying the attention, but who didn't want to appear to be won over too easily.

'Contessa,' he said when he arrived forty minutes later, 'darling you must try on your wedding dress.'

'No, I can't.'

'Oh go on,' the girls chorused.

'Please,' Matthew begged. Sapphire fetched the dress from my bedroom and I had no choice, I disrobed and Bellanna helped me put it on.

The dress is an outrageous dream. Very short and sassy, very *décolletée*, with frills on the bum and a long, long trail.

'It's superb, Contessa. A dream dress, a dress made in heaven. Any dissenters?'

'Dissenters?'

'Do we all agree that the Contessa's dress is made in heaven?'

'Yes. Yes,' said Beatrice, Tricky and Sapphire.

Matthew agreed to read Soloman's Song on my wedding day and we stayed up chatting until two, and then Tricky said we should go to a new club called Xerox, somewhere near to Hanover Square. Matthew grumbled that he was far too old for clubs and decided to go to bed in the spare room.

We ordered a cab and went to Xerox and raved through the night, oblivious, well not quite oblivious, to the nods and winks and stares from several men and wide-eyed girls. I was still in my dress which made me feel so glamorous and wicked. I danced a little, holding on to Sapphire and Beatrice's shoulders and the rest of the time I chatted to Tricky who was hunched up on a banquette smoking joints and refusing to dance because she said the music was naff, not that I thought it was.

I caught a bit of the trail of the dress in the cab door on the way home. Thank God it's not torn.

I have spent the day talking to the caterers, the vicar, a hairdresser and a Sloane woman from a party organisation. Tricky has found a band called

137

the Wicked Wankers. The lead singer, a boy named Ant, telephoned this afternoon, reverse charge, and said he would be arriving tomorrow evening to set everything up and test the sound and perhaps have a short rehearsal. I panicked about where to put them to sleep, but he said they would crash in their van.

Stella, of course, has done nothing, she's still in London, suffering, she says, from a mild form of agoraphobia. May is being angelic, busy organising flowers. She is exhausted, and nodded out this evening over drinks. GC is arriving tomorrow night.

Nev telephoned a minute ago. He made me laugh. He said he was having an early night to prepare for his role as official unofficial photographer. I miss him and wish he was here.

January 27th

Woke up feeling slothful and blue, convinced that I could not go through with the wedding. May was at my bedside asking what colour napkins we should choose for dinner. 'I like the lilac myself,' she said. 'It goes with my hat.'

'Fine,' I said, kissing her and flopping backwards with a huge sigh. The telephone rings non-stop. I'm counting the seconds until Sapphire arrives. I'm not getting up before lunch.

Sapphire and I smoked a joint and then put flowers in all the bedrooms, white, wedding lilies. At about five I had a mild panic attack and kept losing my breath. Sapphire comforted me by saying I could always file for divorce if things don't work out.

I telephoned Nev and he said, 'Elope with me.'

'It would be good,' I said.

'Why not do it, then?'

'I just can't,' I said, thinking of his one-room flat and his mothy appearance and wild electric hair.

'Just a thought,' he said. 'See you tomorrow. By the way,' he said, 'did you know that your fiancé is an arms dealer?'

'He's not.'

'That's what I heard anyway.'

'I have to go,' I said.

January 28th

I'm writing this on the morning of the wedding. Last night both sets of parents were here, as well as Giancarlo's best man who is such a nerd. He instigated some kind of macho drinking competition with GC, and then Dad joined them and later made an emotional toast to his beloved only daughter. Then he grabbed Giancarlo by the arm and asked him if he would take care of me. He asked again, before Giancarlo had had a chance to reply.

'I think I can take care of Anna,' Giancarlo said. 'Probably better than you have.' Dad laughed, thinking GC was joshing. I left the room ready for bed but I couldn't sleep and Sapphire and I spent most of the night chatting downstairs. I confided that Giancarlo and I have only made love once or twice during our engagement, and that is partly because of my leg and partly because he's been away so much, but the awful truth is that when he touches me I usually feel a deep sense of boredom and abstract irritation.

139

Half an hour to go. My heart is beating very fast. Panic palpitations. The palms of my hands are sweaty.

I was standing in my bra and pants, with a blob of bleach on my upper lip when the man who is making the video zoomed into my bedroom. I screamed and knocked over a vase. The man backed out, bumping into Dad who was swaying in the corridor. Dad came in and hugged me. 'Bloody video, who the hell had that idea?'

'Not me,' said Dad. 'You look wonderful.'

'Dad, I can't do it,' I said.

'No,' he said, 'not in your underwear.'

The Italian nerd is knocking on the door. 'Hurry. Everyone waiting.'

January 30th

The wedding ring is on my finger. I am in a trance of exhaustion, lying comatose by the pool next to our rented honeymoon house in the West Indies. We woke up at five this morning because of the four-hour time difference and at eight we went down to the harbour with the cook, to buy some fish from the fishermen who were sitting around untangling huge nets. GC says that in East Caribbean dollars he is a millionaire several times over.

By eight thirty the island was buzzing with brown, buoyant, couples, zipping around in fluorescent mini mokes. GC and I are flaccid and grey in comparison.

We arrived in Barbados after an eight-hour flight yesterday afternoon. The heat hit full force as we stepped on to the aeroplane steps, rather like opening an oven door to check the chicken. A steel band was playing in a fitful fashion on the paved area outside the airport. Once inside the building I lit up, desperate for a cigarette, but was immediately reprimanded by a man in a military uniform, who pointed to the no smoking sign.

I then went outside and sat on a bench in front of the band who by this point had given up any pretence of playing. I lit my second cigarette and managed to inhale one puff before another armed

141

and uniformed man walked over and said I could not wait outside and ordered me to put out my cigarette. I was fuming, a nicotine addict deprived of a fix.

We hung around waiting for a small plane to take us to Papaya Island which is basically a resort for rich whites. When at last we were ushered on board, there was another delay, because a large lady could not get the seat belt around her vast stomach and the pilot had to disembark and help her. Once we were in the air I became fascinated by the clouds. Some were like puffs of stiffened egg-white, light and fluffy while others were more dense and grey, unilluminated by the sun and actually quite dark and eerie and claustrophobic, like passing through hell.

Dad and I had a giggling argument walking up the aisle. He whispered that I was walking too fast and I said he was walking too slowly. Then we became hysterical, silently giggling without being able to move at all. The congregation began to cough. I scanned the crowd looking for Nev, but couldn't see him anywhere. GC was standing by the altar looking grave, but as we got nearer he smiled and I warmed to him.

The party was quite good fun. GC made an impromptu speech, half in Italian. The Italian contingent laughed loudly at the Italian bits, so maybe he is amusing in Italian. GC thanked everyone and blew kisses and then kissed me. Sweet really. Nev and I grabbed a few moments together in the library. He hugged me for a long time, until someone opened the door, a man who said, 'Oh sorry,' in a surprised and rather patronising tone, before closing it again.

February 4th

Breakfast is delivered to each guest-house by men on bicycles bearing a tray in their left hand – mango, papaya with a piece of lime, or grapefruit, and croissants sent over from Martinique. Giancarlo has already been up for hours by the time breakfast arrives, scanning faxes sent by his secretary. Why can't he relax?

He finds it hard to sit still. Even when he's sunbathing, he's moving his legs in a bicycle movement, or otherwise he lies by the pool doing press-ups before rolling into the water and swimming fast for fifty lengths without stopping.

February 5th

Giancarlo was quite annoyed that I asked Darnley, the boy who brings breakfast, where I could get some grass. He appeared an hour later with three ready-rolled joints and whispered that he knew where to get some top level cocaine. We spent the afternoon at a beach on the Atlantic side of the island. It was perfectly empty. I finally persuaded Giancarlo to take a couple of puffs of grass. He inhaled and had a coughing fit, but later he mellowed and we lay silently side by side, holding hands, mesmerized by the awesome sound of the waves rolling back and forth.

This evening we had dinner with a man who publishes Italian *Vogue*. Giancarlo introduced me as his wife, I felt like a possession. 'My name is Anna,' I said, a moment too late, and it sounded rather silly, as

143

though I was trying too hard to make a point, which I was. Uma Thurman was there with her lover and they gave each other looks, glances loaded with desire.

The likelihood of Giancarlo having me anywhere but bed is unlikely, although he did kiss me rather passionately on the beach this morning.

Someone, I can't remember who, told me that Giles had left Dorset and gone off to crew a ship in the West Indies. I dread the idea of seeing him standing at the beach bar laughing in that way he does, without opening his mouth.

February 6th

Our last day. We shopped till we dropped at the boutique. I shopped and Giancarlo paid. He likes long skirts which reveal a hint of leg, and off the shoulder tops, but I bought a white Gottex bikini which looks more like an expensive bra and pants. Afterwards we sat down at the café and looked out at the boats bobbing on the bay. The sky was streaked shades of red, the palm trees waved in the soft wind and the light was fading fast. The sun, large and luminous, balanced for a moment on the horizon like a red beach-ball before literally plunging into the sea. Giancarlo missed it all. He was reading a two-week-old copy of *The Economist*.

February 10th

I'm in London alone. Giancarlo was here for two hours before his secretary telephoned and said something important had come up — something about a share certificate — and he had to return immediately, via Rome.

Why am I melancholic? Doug and I discussed depression once. He told me that health and characteristic mood may be governed by substances that flow through the body, like phlegm, blood and bile, and this belief predates the earliest Greek medical texts. Melan-cholia is Greek for black bile. He said that I am probably drowning in black bile and then he laughed.

My melancholia is nothing to do with black bile or blue mood, it's just the way I've always been, my experience of life. Today we flew first class, and Enrico picked us up and carried our bags. It was all very luxurious, but hardly real. I feel like a rotten egg in a box, gift-wrapped with beautiful and expensive paper and the finest ribbon money can buy.

Maria tactfully waited until Giancarlo had left before telling me that Nev had telephoned three times. I dialled half his number last night, but stopped myself because I am worried that the telephone may be bugged. Giancarlo telephoned today while I was having lunch with Matthew Clivesmith at Luigi's.

145

'Giancarlo!' I said as he announced himself. 'How did you find me here?'

'A big guess. Lunchtime it must be Luigi's.' I laughed, but the point is I don't go to Luigi's that often.

When I sat down I noticed a sinister looking man wearing a scarf hunched up at another table reading a newspaper and glancing in my direction.

'My God, Matthew,' I whispered. 'Look. No don't look now, but there is a man over there wearing a mac. No, not there. There on his own by the window. He's glancing at me. OK, look now. He must be a private detective, hired by Giancarlo, how else would he know I'm here?'

Matthew turned around and then back to me, laughing hysterically. 'Anna,' he snorted, 'Anna, darling, steady on. You're not serious.'

'I am.'

'Don't you think you are being just a little paranoid? I mean Giancarlo is charming, well mannered and rich, but hardly an original. He's not likely to do something quite so outlandish.'

We snorted and laughed and everyone began to look round. 'Matthew,' I said, 'Matthew, seriously, what shall I do? It doesn't feel right, we're not compatible. The marriage is doomed. What shall I do?'

'You don't need to be compatible to spend all that money, darling.'

'But marrying someone you're not really in love with is like stitching up a wound. You feel better for a while, but then you become conscious of the scar and it begins to itch, all the bloody time.'

146

'Scratch. Take a lover. Someone like him.' A young, blond boy with a cherub complexion sat down at the table next to ours. 'Heaven on a stick,' Matthew sighed under his breath.

February 13th

Nev telephoned today. 'What's happening?' he asked. 'Where have you been? Can I see you?'

'I'm not sure,' I said. 'I mean it's hard to talk.'

'Why?'

'Well, I'm married.'

'So . . . Does that mean you can't see a friend?'

'No, but you know,' I persisted. 'You know what I mean.'

'If you imagine for a moment that I have designs on you, you're wrong.'

'Oh,' I said, sounding disappointed, and then he laughed.

'Aha,' he said, 'now I know.'

February 14th

Valentine's Day. I received a large bouquet of flowers with no note. Of course I wanted them to be from Nev and I almost went to a call box to ring him. He finally telephoned at about eight, and I asked him if he'd sent anything. 'Flowers,' I whispered, 'are they from you?'

'Maybe,' he said. 'Perhaps.'

'Well are they or not?'

'That's not the kind of question you should be asking,' he said.

147

'So they are from you?'

'I'm not saying.' He's so irritating. I'm meeting him now, but not in his small, mothy flat in case I'm followed.

February 15th

Last night Nev and I wound each other up in a flirtatious kind of way in an Indian restaurant in Westbourne Park Road. I drank a little too much, and then went and sat on his lap. He let me sit there for a while and then stood up, and said, 'No, this cannot be, we cannot go on like this.' It made me desire him, and, despite his mothy appearance, I wanted to kiss him and told him so. He smiled that twisted smile and laughed that wicked laugh and said, 'Mechanics of Desire, my dear.'

Nick telephoned and said he'd sent the flowers. I was very touched and then he said, 'Well, I never gave you a wedding present.' I told him about Nev, and he said, 'You're joking, you're not into him, he looks like a serial killer on the run from Alcatraz.'

I was walking in Kensington Park Road this afternoon when I bumped into a girl I was at school with – Christine Quatt.

'You look glam,' she said. 'What are you up to?'

I wanted to confide in her, but instead I flashed her my wallet with all the credit cards and giggled, 'I'm a corporate wife. What are you doing?'

'Well, I'm working for an advertising company, just near here. I'm training to be an account director.'

'Brilliant. How eighties,' I said fatuously, laughing.

'Yes,' she smiled her lovely shy smile. 'I do have a mortgage and I work long hours, if that's what you mean.'

We exchanged telephone numbers as old friends who have no intention of ringing each other do. I wrote hers on my cigarette packet. I can imagine what she will say to Cherry Page who she is still in touch with. 'I bumped into Anna. Anna Blaker. She's become a trophy wife, spending someone's money, rushing around in designer clothes, planning dinner parties, having pedicures, that sort of thing.'

I have a vivid memory of Christine – it was winter, early evening, and a group of us were working in the library. I was reading out a sexy, loving, love-letter from my boyfriend. 'You may be in your prime now, Anna,' Christine smiled her lovely shy smile, 'but we'll be in ours later.' That remark used to haunt me when I sat, freezing, in Giles' sitting room, fucked up and depressed. And it haunts me now.

February 20th

Writing this down is good for me, because the rest of my life is a charade. I think I would like to write a story based on the characters I temped for last October. I would call it 'Pig'. It would be about the son who calls himself Pig, ugly as sin, but jolly, his weird dependent relationship with his parents, and his unrequited crush on a girl who works in the office and manipulates him, to make her life easier.

Giancarlo telephoned and said that I am expected in New York in three days' time. He wants me to help him host a dinner for a very important client and the day after we are flying to Vermont to cross country ski with *another married couple*. I can't ski because of my leg, but Giancarlo thinks it is a good place for me to rest. I telephoned Nev at his office, Madco. They said he was out on a mineral drip or something extraordinary.

Nev hasn't called back. Sapphire said my obsession with Nev is mad. She thinks that I am focusing on the first weirdo who comes along to avoid thinking about my own problems. She does have a point, but no one seems to understand that I have a great affection for Nev. It's all right for her. Sapphire is on tip top form because she now has a deal with a publisher, her poems are coming out next year.

February 23rd

Rory Gunn was a thirty-five-year-old man who was known to those who knew him as Pig. He seemed to enjoy his name and dine out on it, not that he did go out to dine very much, but he signed his memos at work with a smiling pig's face. He had been christened Pig at school by a couple of older boys and the name had stuck and caught up with him at college where one of his classmates happened to be doing the same course in business studies.

Pig lived with his parents near Amersham and commuted to work in London's West End every day. He worked for his father as press officer in a small family PR firm. Pig had a fleshy face, small, dull, heavy-lidded eyes, a large protruding nose and dirty reddish hair. He was a plump man and he had a habit of shuffling. He liked to smoke a pipe so his fingers were stained yellow from the tobacco and his breath was always stale. Despite his unfortunate appearance Pig had a jolly disposition – as obese or ugly people usually do – and he liked to hum and sing to himself, 'I'm a fat old Pig, jolly old Pig, kind and nice and sweet old Pig . . .'

The third floor office was shabby, the paint was peeling and the carpet was threadbare. Pig shared the largest room with his father. The windows were never cleaned and a model ship kept in a glass case on Mr Gunn senior's desk was covered in dust, but the biscuit tin was always full. Pig had a habit of rooting around in the tin for the chocolate bourbons.

Alison worked in the office next door. She was employed by Pig's father to work on the French accounts. She was a blonde with pearls. She had a neat, slim figure, packed into perfectly pressed classic clothes. She was a sensible, genial girl and was known to everyone at work as Piglet . . .

I'm writing this Piggy story on my way to New York. Nev has disappeared, he never telephoned me back. He's probably stuck on the mineral drip. I feel anxious that he hasn't called me. Probably something to do with the Mechanics of Desire.

February 24th

Giancarlo collected me at the airport yesterday. He hugged me for a long time and called me baby. We held hands in the back of the limousine. 'Baby,' he said. 'You look very tired.'

'I am,' I said, leaning against him, feeling shattered.

151

'You have been up all night, doing no good.'

'What do you mean?' I asked him.

'Have you been with that druggy-looking man?'

'Who?' I asked, knowing he meant Nev.

'Neville.'

'No, Giancarlo,' I said.

'You have seen him, no?'

'Once,' I said, feeling too weak to lie or fight.

'I don't want you to see him again.'

'Fine, Giancarlo. But I'm only agreeing because you have an uncanny sense of knowing exactly what I am doing, even when you are on the other side of the Atlantic.'

February 29th

Vermont is beautiful and crisp, with fine pine trees and hard sunny snow. The couple are tedious. He's a preppy Harvard graduate, healthy and earnest and completely in awe of Giancarlo and his money. She's not very impressive, except for her teeth, which are very white. She wears a pink snow suit, trimmed with white fur and shows me endless photographs of their 'new holiday home in Connecticut'.

They all get up at eight o'clock, brimming with good will and in excited expectation of the black run, which they cross country ski. I get up at eleven, take a languid bath, lounge over a long breakfast and then take a short walk and meet them for lunch.

Pig's father was nicknamed Badger and his mother Rabbit. Using these appalling animal names in the office was a way of alleviating the boring business of making money. By Wednesday afternoon, Pig was looking forward to the weekend.

Rotund Rabbit came into the office once or twice a week to do the books. Her hair was coarse and dyed an unnatural yellow blonde, which she wore bouffant, piled on top of her head. She liked to wear smock dresses, embroidered with tiny flowers, which she made herself on an old sewing machine. Rabbit's tongue could be sharp and her giggle was raucous. On Rabbit days, Rory Gunn Ltd became a less soporific place to work.

One day, Badger said they needed a girl to work on reception. He had an important new client, and he needed a receptionist. 'Do we really need a new gggggirl?' Pig stammered, feeling a strange mixture of excitement and fear.

'Yes we do son,' Badger replied. 'Piglet needs to spend more time in France. Now get on to an agency, there's a good lad.'

March 2nd

Today the wife, Jenny, offered to stay behind in the afternoon and keep me company. I protested and said I was happy to write my Pig story, but she insisted. We walked around aimlessly, looking at shops. She bought several pots of maple syrup in kitschy boxes while I waited for her at a café, resting my leg. When she joined me she began to talk, meaningless talk about babies, and her husband.

She said that she and Harrison (the hunky husband) have been trying to have a baby for four years. 'We've tried everything, IVF, hypnotherapy,

153

but nothing seems to work. I'm desperate, I feel so unfulfilled. Sometimes when I see a baby buggy, I just want to snatch it.'

'But you wouldn't.'

'Oh no, no, of course not.'

I wanted to say that cute goo-goo babies usually grow up to be drug-taking, cigarette-smoking, snogging adolescents, suspended from their very expensive co-ed schools for rebellious behaviour.

March 3rd

Giancarlo and I had a huge row this morning. I only looked up briefly from my book when Hunky and Pinky came down for breakfast. He said it was rude, insufferable behaviour and it probably was, but I hate the way he admonishes me like a child.

I just telephoned Nev. 'Oh hi,' he said. 'What's happening? Where are you?'

'I'm in Vermont. Where have you been?'

'I've been in the dark room for several days. When are you coming back?'

'Maybe never, maybe soon,' I said, attempting to sound mysterious.

March 7th

Giancarlo and I are flying back to London. Giancarlo will be in London for two days and then he is going to a conference in Brazil. I've already drunk three vodka and tonics. I have an overwhelming urge to get out of my head. Giancarlo thinks I should see a shrink.

*

Pig shuffled and groaned. He hated the telephone, which made his job very difficult. The telephone seemed to make his stutter worse and trapped words in his mouth. He rehearsed what he would say in his head and then softly outloud, but by lunch time he still hadn't made the call. At three o'clock, he dialled the number for Perky People, an agency that Piglet had heard about.

'Perky People, please hold.'

Pig almost hung up, but then the girl came back and said, 'Can I help?' She sounded encouraging.

'Hello, it's Roland GGGGGGGun, from RRRRRRory Gunn Ltd.'

'Yes?'

'We are a public relations company and we are looking for a girl to work on rrrrrrr . . .'

'Reception?'

'Yes,' said Pig gratefully.

The agency sent a girl called Michelle who said she wanted to 'get into PR'. 'I'm very good with people, all sorts, including celebrity types.' Pig could not keep his eyes off her long red fingernails, but she was concentrating on Badger, selling herself hard. Badger sat back in his turnaround leather chair. She really wouldn't do. She looked . . . well, all wrong. She was a bit brash and rather . . . vulgar.

The agency faxed the CV of another girl, Geraldine Harper. She had been to the right sort of school, Badger noticed, and had a permanent address, in a village near to theirs in Buckinghamshire. She wasn't available for interview right away, the agency said, because she was on holiday, but an appointment was made for the week she was expected back. On the

155

day of the intended interview, the agency telephoned to say they couldn't get hold of Geraldine. She hadn't returned. Mr Gunn senior was asked if he would like to see another girl, but he declined the offer and said he would wait for Miss Harper.

March 9th

I had a huge row with GC, because he heard Maria telling me that Nev had telephoned five or six times. He said he was sick and tired of Nev ringing and that he was not a suitable person to have as a friend. Of course that riled me up and I protested that I should be able to choose who my friends were.

The telephone rang, GC picked it up and hung up. 'Who was that?' I asked.

'Your friend. I don't want . . .'

The telephone rang again. We both went to pick it up, and while I struggled to speak, Giancarlo wrestled with me. 'LEAVE IT,' I shouted. At last he conceded but I had to tell Nev I would call him later.

The rest of the evening was awful. Giancarlo sulked and I felt trapped. In the middle of the night, Giancarlo leant over and woke me up. 'I am very upset,' he said. 'We must talk.' In the end, for some odd reason I agreed that I would go and see a shrink, anything to shut him up.

March 11th

Giancarlo has left and we are not meeting again until Easter, in about three weeks' time. I have promised not to see Nev, although it was a rash pledge and I made it under pressure. GC has arranged an appointment for me with a counsellor, a man named Hans who lives somewhere in Hampstead. This morning, however he implored me to accompany him to New York, but I said it was probably more constructive to stay in London and visit Hans.

'You don't want to leave London because of Nev,' Sapphire said on the telephone.

'That's not true. I don't know anyone in New York, what would I do in New York?'

'I'm sure you'd think of something if you really wanted to be with Giancarlo.' She's right of course.

'You're right,' I said, 'but for God's sake don't tell anyone. I've promised not to see Nev.'

'No, I promise,' she said. 'Are you going to see him?'

March 14th

Geraldine Harper sat on the swivel chair in reception. The switchboard was a row of nine white switches with small square lights above them, set into a grey stand. Piglet showed her what to do. When lights one

157

to five flashed, she had to flick the switch up and say, 'Rory Gunn Ltd.' If lights five to ten flashed it would be a call from France. If she had to put the French caller on hold she was instructed to say, 'Ne quitte pas,' which she translated dramatically to herself as 'Don't leave me.'

Pig stood behind her for the first half of the morning, showing her how to deal with the switchboard. When there was a lull, he said, 'Think of an animal name for yourself.'

Geraldine laughed. 'I'm going to make a cup of tea, would you like one?'

'I'll make you one,' he said, 'because I'm a fat, jolly old Pig.'

By Friday, Geraldine was proficient on the switchboard and she had learnt to use the ancient fax – a monster of a machine that needed letters or memos typed directly on to the keyboard. Badger and Pig thought she was doing very well. On Friday afternoon, Pig said, 'You better think of an animal name over the weekend.'

'Yeh,' said Geraldine as they went down the stairs together, 'I will.'

When Geraldine walked in on Monday morning, Pig blushed. She said good morning and walked past him towards the kettle. Pig shuffled after her, the pipe sticking out of his mouth, 'PPPPPPPPPerhaps you could make a cup of tea for BBBBBBBadger.'

'Yeh, I will,' Geraldine said, stuffing a biscuit into her mouth.

'And have you thought of an animal name?' Pig asked, blowing the smoke in her face.

'Oh,' said Geraldine, backing away, 'no I haven't.
158

I completely forgot.'

Pig went back to his office, his body drooped, making him look dejected. When Geraldine knocked on their office door, Badger cried out 'Come in,' and, seeing the cup of tea, he smiled and said, 'Thank you, dear.'

March 15th

I went to see Hans this evening. He's a large, bearded man with a German accent. I was very edgy by the time I found his street and wished I had let Enrico drive me. He had offered, but it seemed a bit spoilt to drag him across London in the rush-hour, when he has such a bad cold. Hans' consulting room was full of silver trophy cups and shelves of psychiatric books. He looked at me for a very long time, at least twenty pounds' worth of silence and then said, 'Vell . . .'

'Um . . . What do you want to know?'

'Why have you come here today?'

'My husband thought it would be a good idea, if I came . . .'

'But vot about you?'

'I'm not sure . . .'

'You are not sure.'

He repeated almost everything I said. I told him that my marriage made me feel trapped and claustrophobic. He said that he had felt the same way when he was newly married. He went on to tell me a long story about how he had met his wife at a language school in London, wasting at least another twenty pounds' worth of time. I never confided in

159

him about my crush on Nev. I'm not so sure I trust him.

When I left Hans' house there was a tramp sitting on the pavement. I fumbled around in my wallet and retrieved a one pound coin. 'Thanks . . . bitch,' he said, which hurt.

March 16th

An interminable Sunday, a dismal, grey day with low cloud. Maria was away for the weekend, and I didn't speak to a soul. I read the newspapers front to back and then back to front and even glanced at the sport and business sections. By six o'clock I couldn't stand my own company for a second longer and I telephoned Nev.

'Oh hi,' he said. 'Where have you been?'

'Here,' I said. 'What about you?'

'I've been in the dark room for days.'

'What do you *do* in the dark room?'

'Work,' he said. 'Do you want to meet for a drink later?'

'Well, well, I don't know, I mean, Giancarlo . . .'

'What about him? Is something amiss?' he asked in a camp, theatrical voice.

'Well, he's jealous, very jealous,' I whispered.

'Of what?'

'You.'

'I see,' he said. 'OK.'

'OK what?'

'OK we won't meet.'

'But I'd like to,' I said.

We arranged to meet in code. I said I would

160

collect him at Moth, meaning his flat.

March 16th

We are in the Portobello Hotel. We checked in last night because it was too late for non-residents to have a drink in the bar. He's still asleep, he's obviously called Nev because he never gets up. He says he loves me but I can't really contemplate a physical relationship, he's just too mothy and dusty. I fear that he may smell of mould.

I'm home now. I didn't check the bill properly, although my heart sank when I saw that it was over £1,000. Nev offered to pay, but of course his credit card was bust. We left at twelve and went for breakfast at a Portuguese café in the Golborne Road. Maria was frenzied by the time I got home.

'Where have you been?' she asked. 'Giancarlo has telephoned three or four times.'

'I stayed the night with a friend,' I said.

'Nev,' she said.

'No, not Nev. With Sapphire.'

'Sapphire, she call just now looking for you.'

'OK, well it's nobody's business where I stay. What did you tell Giancarlo?'

'It's all right,' she said. 'I tell him you are sleeping.'

'Thanks, Maria.'

'Hey,' she said, 'I cannot tell him this every time.'

'No, I know.'

She then asked if she could borrow my new Selina Blow jacket for a party tonight. I was reluctant, because it is a pale lilac colour and Giancarlo gave it

161

to me. 'If anything happened to it, if you spilt some red wine, how would I explain to Giancarlo?'

'If it wasn't for me,' she said, 'you would have to explain many more difficult things.'

She has an uncanny knack of winning an argument. After she managed to get my jacket I noticed that she was wearing my Patrick Cox shoes which I had left out to lend to Sapphire.

'My shoes,' I said feebly.

'Yes, you throw away no . . . ? You cannot throw them away, they are so beautiful. You look great in them, but if you don't want them, I would so love to wear them. It would be the best present you could ever give me.'

March 20th

It's Stella's fiftieth birthday party this weekend. May is giving a party for her. I haven't really spoken to Stella since September when she was such a bitch. I don't really want to compromise myself by going to her birthday party, pretending that nothing is askew between us, but May would like me to be there and that is the point.

March 22nd

Nev telephoned this morning when Maria and I were having a row about my black lace skirt which she borrowed to mourn a cousin and now can't find. 'I'll get back to you,' I said.

'OK,' he said. 'It's urgent.'

'What's happening?' he asked when I got back

162

to him.

'I'm ringing back,' I said.

'Oh, right,' he said. 'I can't talk now, can I call you back?'

We spoke to each other finally at about five and he asked me out for dinner. We went to Maroush, a Lebanese restaurant in Beauchamp Place, where we were lucky to find a couple of stools at the chrome bar, a good position to watch hirsute dark chefs in their white aprons turning over endless cubes of chicken on the grill. We drank cool, fresh melon juice and ate crisp chicken wings smothered in thick, white, garlic sauce and crushed aubergine with warm, flat bread.

While we were drinking mint tea in small glass cups, Nev told me that he wanted to give up design and do photography full-time. I asked him what had happened to the wedding photographs. Giancarlo has demanded to see them four or five times and so has his mother. Nev looked rather annoyed and dismissive when I questioned him and said he'd show me the contacts at the end of the week.

I invited him to Stella's party as my date and then he asked for the bill. He pulled out a handful of change and said, 'God, just about enough money to buy a packet of Benson and Hedges,' but then he found a crumpled twenty-pound note, that had obviously been in his pocket for some time and I paid the difference. There was a paparazzi photographer sitting at the end of the bar, waiting for someone interesting to leave San Lorenzo across the road. I made Nev leave a few minutes before me because you can never be too sure.

March 23rd

Tricky has split up with her boyfriend Rod. Thank God. They were living together and never saw anyone, and it was difficult to even speak to her on the telephone because he always seemed to be in the room. She came over, cried incessantly and telephoned her own answering machine every few minutes to check if there were any messages. When she had exhausted the topic of her boring boyfriend I told her that I had decided to sleep with Nev tonight, despite his appearance. 'You will freak,' she said, 'I know you.'

'Oh come on,' I said. 'He's not that bad.'

'I don't see it,' she said. 'Frankly I don't.'

March 24th

Stella's party last night. I was wearing a low-cut Rifat Ozbek dress, and I had made an effort to put make-up on. Stella was wearing a pair of black crêpe trousers, and a multi-coloured sequinned jacket. She was very over-excited and whipped around the room refilling people's glasses before they had even managed to have one sip.

I went into the kitchen, where May was putting candles on the cake, which was made in two shapes – a six and a zero. 'She's only fifty,' I laughed.

'OH NO,' May giggled. 'Are you sure?'

'Yes.'

'What shall we do?'

'We'll have to get rid of the six,' I said and then

164

we stuffed our faces with it and threw some away, giggling like school girls.

Later I sat in a corner with the professor who told me a sad story about his life as a boy. He was brought up in Canada, and sent to boarding school. He was a brainy boy and he had a best friend, a swot named Jenkins. On Sundays when the boys were sent off in twos for a picnic in the grounds, the professor paired off with Jenkins. Then one day another boy arrived at the school: Wigram was not only brainy but good-looking, a talented sportsman and a clever mimic. Wigram seduced Jenkins away from the professor and became his rival in Latin and maths.

The professor mourned the loss of his friend. Sundays were never quite the same. Jenkins now went off with Wigram for the picnic. 'I never enjoyed school after that,' he said in his upturned, high-pitched voice.

'That's the saddest story I've ever heard,' I said.

The professor laughed his parrot-laugh. 'Oh, it's not that bad. Not that bad.'

It was the longest conversation I have ever had with the professor, and I found it quite enlightening. It probably explains why he is such a loner, and can't cope with social situations unless he is soaked in drink. I think May likes him because he adores her and indulges her with praise and lets her get away with murder.

As he was talking I kept one eye on the door, waiting for Nev. Every time the door-bell rang, my stomach lurched a little. Finally Stella stumbled towards me, 'Someone here for you.' I ran to the front door. Nev was standing there with a girl.

'I've brought Layla,' he said, pointing at the young,

165

dark girl with large eyes. 'I bumped into her.'

'I'm sorry,' she said. 'He told me to come. I hope it's all right.'

I was speechless. The name Layla was familiar. He had mentioned her once when we were talking about ex-lovers.

'Come in,' I said frostily. I introduced Nev to May, but didn't bother introducing Layla.

'What's the matter?' he asked, grabbing me. 'Come in here with me,' he said, pulling me towards the bathroom.

'Why did you bring her?' I asked.

'No reason. I bumped into her,' he said. 'I didn't think you would mind.'

'I don't particularly mind, but it's not my party, it's my mother's and you are meant to be my date,' I said childishly. 'And I thought you were going to take some photographs.'

'Yeh,' he said, 'yeh, well, look, my cameras are not insured at the moment so I don't think it's a good idea to bring them out with me. But I'll go right now. If you want me to.'

'Fine,' I said.

'Fine,' he said. 'I'll go.'

Just before he left, the girl, Layla, bumped into me in the bedroom as she was getting her coat. 'I'm not his girlfriend you know,' she said. 'I used to be, but not any more.'

'I know,' I said, lightly, dismissing the situation as if I didn't care.

The whole scene was so humiliating, particularly as I had imagined sleeping with the mouldy moth. I dialled Giancarlo's number. 'Count di Trevi's office,'
166

Tracey whined. 'Can I help you?'

'It's Anna.'

'Hello, Countess di Trevi.'

'Please call me Anna,' I said, maybe a little too curtly. 'Is my husband there?'

'He's here, but like he's on a conference call right now. Can I take a message?'

'Yes. Can you ask him to call me. I'll give you the number.'

I waited around for Giancarlo to ring back. I drank more and more, avoiding Stella's eye. When GC did finally ring I was drunk.

'Giancarlo. Let's meet in Spain before Easter. I miss you. I love you.'

'What is it?' Giancarlo laughed. 'I have a feeling of suspicion.'

Oh God, I thought. He can't take me being loving. 'No reason to be suspicious, I just want to be with you in bed, now.'

'Me too.'

'Right. Well, why don't you make it to Spain a few days early? Please, darling. London is really getting me down.'

'I will see what I can do,' he said.

March 27th

It's warm. I'm sitting by the pool reading a book called *Hideous Kinky*. I bought it at the airport because I love the title. We are just outside Marbella, in La Virginia, an 'urbanacion' designed to look like a traditional Andalusian village. The streets are cobbled, the windows shuttered and there are geranium pots hanging off the balconies. The houses have been built around the existing trees. GC's partner has lent us the house in return for letting him stay in GC's flat in Rome. Nothing could be more heavenly than reading a good book while the sun shines, although frankly I'd rather be in Rome.

We arrived this morning at Malaga Airport and rented a huge Mercedes. Giancarlo has the rather irritating habit of driving either too fast or too slowly. Too slowly on the motorway and too fast in town. We drove past Torremolinos, an unattractive blot on the landscape, particularly the proliferation of highrise towers spreading like a contagious disease along the coast. I can't stop thinking about the untreated sewage dumped in the sea. British tourists swimming around in digested chicken, chips and tepid lager.

GC annoyed me in the car. He said my skin was looking dry and asked me if I was using moisturiser on my face. I replied that I do wear moisturiser, a

168

very expensive one with vitamin E and all sorts of sun-filters. So then he said, 'Well, it must be the cigarettes. Very bad for the skin. How many do you smoke a day?'

'I've no idea,' I said.

'Twenty a day.'

'No, not twenty. It depends. Sometimes I only smoke five, but if I'm going to a party, maybe I'll smoke ten.'

'Too many.'

I sighed and then looked around the damn car for the right switch to open the window. I lit a cigarette. He smacked my hand playfully and I wanted to smash him in the face.

March 28th

Last night we hooked up with an oil man who lives next door. He's American, very rich, middle-aged, a big drinker, with a big stomach. His name is Don. We drove into Puerto Buenos for a drink and sat at a café in the port, watching all the people walking by. The women are far too glitzy and glittery for my taste – sparkling shoes, tight lycra, sequinned jackets. Don the American made lewd comments about the mini clingy dresses.

He told me a candid story about how he picks up young oriental girls when he's in London. He goes to Harvey Nichols food store and loiters around the Japanese spices. He spots a young Japanese girl on her own, says a few words to her in Japanese, and then asks her what a certain spice or herb is. 'How do you cook it?' he probes, moving in. She tells him, then he strikes – 'Well, actually I'm having a dinner tonight, why don't you come?'

Giancarlo was smoking a cigar and the smoke was blowing in my face. I was drinking hot chocolate and feeling guilty about it. Suddenly a large crowd gathered outside one of the boats docked in the port.

'Must be someone famous on board,' Don said. Several macho policemen were swimming around with menacing looks on their faces.

'Prince or someone,' I said.

Don and I walked towards the crowd, while Giancarlo remained seated, reading the *Herald Tribune*. We were told they were waiting for a glimpse of Julio Iglesias's daughter. Frankly, it really is the end.

March 29th

We went to the Easter Parade in Malaga – Semana Santa. A procession of 'penitants' wearing white, black or purple Ku Klux Klan-type costumes with pointed hoods walked slowly past, some had bare feet. They were carrying floats on their shoulders: alabaster versions of Our Lady crying or Our Lady resplendent, scenes of Christ on the cross and one of Pontius Pilate having his hands washed. The men had to stop every few paces and put the heavy floats down, recover for a moment and then pick them up again.

GC and I are getting on remarkably well. I'm making more of an effort because Giancarlo is such a good man and the sun is making me feel benign and sexy. We have four-hour afternoon siestas behind

shuttered windows and give each other long, lan-
guorous massages with suntan oil and then slowly
make love. Giancarlo has never been so relaxed and
I think it is because business is going well and he's
just made a fortune selling a small Caravaggio at
auction, inherited from his grandfather. I wish he'd
kept it, but GC said the insurance premium would
have been too high to be able to hang it on a wall.

March 30th

Last night we went to the Marbella Club for dinner with a friend of Giancarlo's, a woman named
Consuelo Head of a Cow, (her surname translated).
She lives in Madrid and is a spectacular snob. She
bored on about how difficult it is to infiltrate into
Spanish aristocratic society. She looks like a thousand other women, streaked blonde hair, tanned skin,
crooked teeth and red, lipsticked lips. She's invited us
to Madrid for the weekend. Giancarlo says he'd like
to go although he wants to stay at the Ritz.

The Marbella Club is pink, pink, pink. I kept expecting to see one of the Collins sisters perched on the
bar-stool drinking Pink Gin or Dame Barbara Cartland
powdering her nose in the loo. The poor old men
were wearing trousers with high waistbands, pastel-
coloured shirts and odd-looking golf-type shoes. The
wives wore too much make-up and dresses patterned
with flowers of hideous turquoise and yellow. They
sat around drinking large glasses of gin and blowing
smoke in each other's faces.

Giancarlo has bought one of those new mobile
telephones that can receive calls from all over the

world. It means bubble-gum Tracey is in constant touch. She's organised for him to pick up some money from a bank in Gibraltar tomorrow and collect a few faxes and he's asked me to accompany him to that boring old rock.

March 31st

We are back from the rock and I'm in terrible trouble. Tracey faxed copies of bills paid. GC received his Visa card statement.

'What is this?' he asked me. '£1,400 at the Portobello Hotel. Is this you?'

'No,' I said, then realised that I wouldn't get away with it. 'Oh yes,' I said, 'that must have been the time that Sapphire's boiler broke down and she had no heating or hot water, but one night *can't* have cost £1,400.'

'Maybe there is a mistake,' GC said. 'Why didn't you ask her to stay at the flat?'

'I don't know,' I said, 'we had dinner there and just ended up staying.'

'Really, Anna, that is too much of an extravagance.'

'I'm sorry, Giancarlo,' I said. 'You're right, I was far too extravagant, but there really must have been a mistake.' The whole incident has truly freaked me out and given me a fright, and I feel guilty.

April 1st

Very embarrassing today. We went to a lunch party given by Don. The women all looked the same — blonde highlighted hair, tanned and slightly wrinkled décolletage, ex-wives of somebody famous or dead. I sat next to a man dressed in white who is going to be coaching tennis for the summer season at the Marbella Club. I told him I had been to Gibraltar yesterday. 'What's it like?' he asked.

'It's horrible,' I said. 'Absolutely horrible. Crowded with ugly people wearing hideous shorts and eating ice-cream. It's like Merton High Street in the sun.'

'I'm from Merton,' he said.

'Oh are you?' I said brightly, wanting to die. 'What's it like?'

'Like Gibraltar under cloud,' he said, smiling.

April 3rd

Very hot today. I telephoned Sapphire but she was a bit off with me.

'Look, in case Giancarlo asks,' I said, 'we stayed together at the Portobello Hotel one night because your boiler broke down, the night I was there with Nev.'

'*Anna*, that really makes me look like a spoilt cow.'

'I'm sorry. But it makes me look like a spoilt cow, not you.'

'God,' she said, 'why do I have to be an alibi for your extra marital affairs? By the way, I saw Nev last night.'

'Did you? Where?'

'He was at Dominique's opening.'

'Did you talk to him?'

'Yeh. He asked me why I was ignoring him.'

'Did he say anything about me?'

'Um . . .' God I thought, how could she forget

something as important as this. 'Um . . . I don't think
so. Oh yes, he asked me if I'd seen you.'

'What did you say?'

'I said you were in Spain.'

'Did he ask when I was coming back?'

'No, that was it. You weren't mentioned again.'

'Was he with anyone?'

'Um . . .' There was another long pause. 'Another
man,' she said finally. 'By the way, Beatrice is quite
annoyed with you. Something about you nicking her
address book.'

April 4th

Last night I couldn't sleep because I was worrying
about the bill at the Portobello Hotel. We did have
a few drinks, and a few snacks. Perhaps we had a
couple of bottles of champagne and quite a few
glasses of whisky, but surely not £1,400 worth.

Today GC, Don and I had lunch with an Australian
painter who lives in a village called Gaucin, about an
hour and a half's drive from here up in the hills. The
day was spoilt for me because in the afternoon we
saw some kids pulling a small bull through the streets
with a rope. They were taunting it and prodding it
with a large stick to make it run, while a thin, scraggy
dog snapped at its heels.

We drove back in the dark, down the long moun-
tain track, when suddenly the tyre punctured. Don
and GC pretended they knew what they were doing
with the jack while I stood by the side of the road like
a flaky babe. We all laughed and laughed, but after
half an hour of getting nowhere we slightly lost our

sense of humour, particularly GC who had to wipe his black grease-stained hands on his newly-pressed cream, linen handkerchief. Help arrived in the form of a truck rattling down the road. Don waved it down and explained in a mixture of bad Spanish and a great deal of miming what had happened. The truck reversed so that the headlights beamed full on to our tank-like car. Then a man and his son, (even I understood that much), fixed it in a matter of moments.

GC and Don stood by awkwardly, watching the man and his son intently. I continued to lean on the side of the car, staring at the stars. Being a girl has its good moments and one of them is not having to feign interest in car dramas. GC gave the man a wad of pesetas which was slightly embarrassing, although perhaps I am being too sensitive.

April 6th

Here we are in Madrid. GC has managed to fix up a couple of meeting with somebody about something. He is very annoyed that the Ritz is full. We are staying in the Palace Hotel, with its glitzy ritzy reception. Imagine, just imagine if I had gone off with Nev. Where would I be now? Probably in that seedy room in Notting Hill, with the patterned shirts hanging to dry on a rack that stands over the grungy bath, cricket on the television, drug-dealers banging on the door.

I'm sitting in a café eating *jambon* sandwiches and a dish of potato and sausage. GC has gone somewhere for a meeting. I'm going to write some more of the Pig story, which I've been neglecting lately.

It was half way through Geraldine's third week at Rory Gunn Ltd. She returned from lunch break and Pig asked her if she would go to the post office and buy stamps for the office. He showed her where the petty cash box was kept and asked her to bring back a receipt. Pig sat down at reception because Piglet was out at lunch. He hummed to himself, 'I'm a fat old Pig, jolly old Pig, kind and nice and sweet old Pig.'

A light was flicking on the switchboard. Pig answered. 'RRRRory Gunn Ltd.'

'Geraldine Harper please.' It was a man with a confident and brisk manner. 'SSShe's not here,' Pig stuttered. 'CCCan I help?'

'I wouldn't have thought so,' the man said. 'It's Pig, isn't it? Tell her that Peter called.'

'Yes, dddoes she . . .' The man had hung up.

Pig was rather taken aback. He had never been called Pig by a stranger before. Not even Geraldine had called him Pig, although he wished she would. Was this man her boyfriend? His stomach felt as if it was falling out. She had never mentioned a boyfriend. He wrote her a note: Please call Peter. He signed with a Pig face, a sad old Pig face with a down-turned mouth. But he thought better of it and scrunched up the note and started again. This time he signed with the fat old Pig, jolly old Pig's smiling face.

Piglet arrived back laden down with bags of shopping. 'Golly I'm tired,' she said. 'What's happened to Geraldine?'

176

Pig looked at his watch, it was over half an hour since she'd left. 'She went to buy some stamps . . . Piglet?'

'Yes, Pig.' Piglet was smiling.

'Does Geraldine have a boyfriend?'

Piglet was fiddling with her pearls. 'Um. I think there is a chap.'

'What's his name?'

'Um.' Piglet scrunched up her eyes. 'I think he's called Peter. Why?'

'NNNNNNothing,' Pig said.

Pig stood up, puffing on his pipe. He sat down at the fax and studied a letter his father wanted sent to France. The spider scrawl was always hard to decipher. He hit his pudgey fingers on the keyboard and finished the first sentence. He stretched, turned around and saw that a light on the switchboard was flashing.

Pig muttered something under his breath. He would have to abandon the fax and start again later. He flicked up the switch and picked up the receiver.

'Is Geraldine back yet?' The voice was instantly recognisable, confident and brusque. It was that man Peter. 'She's not back yet,' Pig said, 'I'll tell her you called again.'

'Thanks, Pig.'

'Actually my name is . . . ' But Peter had hung up.

Geraldine returned to the office ten minutes later. 'I'm sorry,' she said, 'there was a long queue and three people pushed ahead of me. And just as I got to the head of the line, the man said the section was closed.'

'That's all right,' said Pig. 'Your boyfriend called twice.'

177

'Boyfriend?'

Pig handed her the note.

Geraldine blushed. 'He's not really my boyfriend.'

'Oh,' said Pig, 'well, he called me Pig.'

'Did he?' Geraldine laughed.

'Yes he did. It was rather odd.'

'I told him about the office, you see,' Geraldine said.

'Right,' said Pig. Geraldine had sat down and Pig stood above her puffing on the pipe.

'I'd better call him then,' Geraldine said, throwing the Piggy note away.

I walked back to the hotel. The sun was scorching. A young couple stood on the steps. The girl had high cheekbones and a conceited expression. Her hair was tied back, stretched smooth. Hard, proud, nipples protruded through her cream-coloured silk shirt. Her boyfriend had a tanned arrogant face. He wore a well-cut light suit. He helped the girl on with her jacket but she did not smile or thank him. I was sure that she had never spent the night on a dog-haired yellow sofa, or been obsessed with someone like Nev or lived amidst a pile of washing up in a cottage that was as cold as a larder.

The concierge gave me a nod and a half a smile. I sauntered over. Giancarlo's friend who works in the Italian embassy in Paris told me that whenever he is in a strange city he befriends the concierge. 'In every city,' he said, 'I know a concierge. The concierge is like my father.'

'Where do you want to go to?' the concierge asked me.

178

'Um . . . the old part.'

He was a small man with oily hair. There was something so reassuring about the way he smoothed out the map on the cool marble surface and marked a square around the hotel with a red felt-tip pen. 'You go up the hill,' he said, drawing a line through the Puerto de Sol, past la Plaza Mayor and on to the Old Palace.

Later I left my new dark glasses on a table in the Plaza Mayor where I had stopped to quench my thirst, drinking three Coca Colas in quick succession. I had been sitting for a while admiring the muralled palace and wishing a group of gum-chewing American students would vanish. Their loose, whiny voices jarred, trashing the moment and polluting the sunny air. I went to pay the bill.

'How much is that?' I can say it in Italian and French, but couldn't think of the Spanish. I held out a palmful of change, hoping the man would take the right amount.

'You're not British are you?' It was a northern male voice, a man sandwiched between two voluptuous Spanish girls.

'No,' I said, wondering perhaps naïvely, what he was doing with two pretty girls.

'Best thing to do,' he said, 'is to stand in front of the till and watch the figures.'

I left the café. Half-way back to the hotel, I remembered the glasses, lying on the table, but instead of turning around and going back I walked into a shop and bought another pair. I am aware that in another life, BG (before Giancarlo), I would have run desperately back to that café, swearing, sweating

179

and out of breath to claim the lost ones. But now I behave like the girl with the glacial allure.

April 7th

Last night we went to the Bar Cock with Ms Head of a Cow. 'This is a bar,' she said, 'for artists, models and people who look over their shoulders.' It was hard to find, this bar for glamorous people. It was in a side street, behind an inconspicuous door, but inside, the room was huge with wood-panelled walls. Behind the bar three shelves packed with coloured bottles of different shapes and sizes were reflected in a mirrored wall. We sat on a leather banquette and ordered gin fizzes and then some more.

Ms Head of a Cow told us there were no large American-style supermarkets in Madrid. 'Let's open one,' GC said. He was a little drunk.

'Yes,' I said, playing along, 'we'll open a chain of Di Trevi's and become multi-millionaires.'

'It's such a good idea,' said Head of a Cow, placing her hand lightly on Giancarlo's thigh. He didn't push it away and she didn't remove it.

'Time to go,' I said to GC.

'Yes,' he said, standing up. 'I am very tired.'

She said she would stay a while, there was a crowd of people she knew on the other side of the room. He kissed her on her forehead and said goodnight. I said nothing, maybe I mumbled good night, but I certainly didn't kiss her.

'Did you see that?' I asked him later in bed, 'the way she had her hand on your thigh?'

'No,' he said, 'not true.'

180

'It is, Giancarlo.' I saw it. 'Do you fancy her?'

'No,' he said. 'Not really.'

'What do you mean not really. That implies that you do a bit.'

'I mean, she's not ugly, but I don't find her madly attractive.'

'But she fancies you,' I said.

'No,' he said, kissing me, 'no, she's married to a very grand and very rich man.'

'But not happy,' I said. 'Obviously. Where is her husband?'

'He travels,' said Giancarlo. 'He has business in Argentina.'

'Business or mistress.'

'Business,' said GC. 'Most definitely.'

This morning the concierge asked me if I had been to the Prada. 'Oh my God, no,' I said, 'and our flight is after lunch.'

'You must go, now,' he urged me. 'Not too far from here.' He whipped out another map, smoothed it out on the marble surface and drew a red square around the museum. I called the room.

'Giancarlo, we have to go to the Prada, now.'

'Not possible,' he said. 'I am waiting for a telephone call. And it is too late to rush here and there. We leave the hotel in forty minutes.'

Of course *business* first. He would never sacrifice a telephone call for one of the most important galleries in the world. The fact annoyed me intensely. I loved the tall cool galleries and the awesome Valázquezs. I walked briskly, wondering how many other people had to see the Prada in less than half an hour.

As I was passing the early Goyas I overheard a

181

middle-aged American couple discussing a painting. 'I don't really like this artist,' the woman said to her husband.

'Who is it?' he asked, adjusting his baseball cap.

'Goya,' she replied, peering at the plaque.

'Oh Goya,' he said. 'Well,' he paused, 'the artist doesn't like you if you don't like him.'

Wouldn't it be wonderful if all relationships were that simple.

April 10th

Maria hasn't returned from holiday. I think she went to a Greek island with someone. It's unfortunate that she is not here, because Giancarlo is not at his best with mess. He looks murderous when he sees a pile of my clothes on the back of the chair, or a discarded towel on the bedroom floor.

'Anna,' he said as he was leaving today, 'don't forget to make the bed.'

I wanted to kill him, because it reminded me of my mother. 'Clean up that pig-sty of a room,' she used to shout at me.

I had a strange dream last night. I dreamt that I was on holiday with Sapphire, somewhere hot. Daniel Day-Lewis had rented the house next to ours and she fell in love with one of his friends, another achingly good-looking actor. She was whisked off her feet and I hardly saw her again. In the dream I was very anxious and pained, and felt miserably deserted. When I woke up, it was with a huge sense of relief.

It's an anxiety dream. Obviously, I don't need a session with Hans to work that one out. I'm obviously concerned that Sapphire is having her poems published next year, while I lag behind, achieving less than nothing. What can I do? If I don't establish a career soon, his parents will be nagging at me to produce some grandchildren. I've seen my cousin Caro endlessly wiping up milky puke and disposing of shit. Oh God.

Dramas with Beatrice and Ivan Greenburg. Apparently Ivan hasn't received his new American Express card and in his typical paranoic state suspects one of us of stealing it. Frankly. He's put a photocopied letter through everyone's post-box, alerting us all to the drama and last night he knocked on the door. Giancarlo answered.

'Excuse me for asking,' I heard Greenburg say, 'but are you sure you and your wife both have your own credit cards?'

'Of course,' Giancarlo said politely.

'Would you mind if I checked?' Ivan asked.

'Yes, I would,' Giancarlo answered. 'And I don't like your suspicious tone.'

'Well, your wife, she . . . there is the matter of . . . the stolen milk bottle.'

'I am afraid I cannot continue this conversation without my solicitor being present. You have implied that my wife may be involved with a stolen milk bottle and you suspect the inhabitants of this building may have committed fraud with your credit card. It is outrageous. Good night,' he said, shutting the door.

'Well done, Giancarlo,' I said, hugging him.

'And what is the matter of the stolen milk bottle?' Giancarlo laughed.

'It was a moment of desperation,' I replied.

The drama with Beatrice is absurd. The notebook drama. I took a notebook to Paris when we all went there over Christmas. In the book I had scribbled ideas for a couple of short stories and I had written

184

a few paragraphs of the Pig story. For some reason I left the book at Beatrice's house when we dropped her off in London and she adopted it as an address book. I kept forgetting to get it off her and when at last I went round to her house and saw it on a table I put it in my bag. Now she has accused *me* of stealing *her* address book.

We had a heated telephone conversation. She accused me of stealing her book. I defended myself by saying it was mine originally. She asked me to get it back to her immediately, but I said I was too busy to bring it round, so she asked me to send it over in a taxi. 'Oh, FUCK OFF,' I said, slamming the telephone down. There is something about Beatrice that makes me want to behave like a madwoman, perhaps it is her imperious spoilt tone, which she sometimes adopts when she feels she has been wronged. We won't be talking for a very long time.

April 13th

I dreamt that Nev was beside me in the bed. When I woke up I felt a deep sense of loss and disappointment that he wasn't really there. The bed was empty, Giancarlo had gone off for a breakfast meeting. He had left me a note: Anna. Please tidy and wash up before I return. It enraged me. I grabbed the last clean bowl, tipped in some branflakes, peeled a banana, and with my mouth still full, dialled Nev's number.

'Oh hi,' he said. 'Where have you been?'

'Here and there.'

'How long have you been back?' he asked.

'A week,' I lied.

'Oh I see,' he said in his camp theatrical voice. 'Well, when are we going to meet?'

'I don't know that we can,' I said, 'and anyway what about your girlfriend?'

'Girlfriend?' he asked in an exaggerated quizzical way.

'Layla, the girl you asked to my mother's fiftieth birthday party. The night you were meant to be a photographer and my date . . . You bastard.'

By this time I had worked myself up into quite a state. 'Look, I've got to go,' I said. 'Goodbye.'

My heart was beating. I sat on the bed, hoping he would call back and mollify me. I lay on the bed, staring at the ceiling. At last I sat up and flicked through a copy of the *Spectator*, and fantasised about writing a column entitled 'Lazy Life'. Waiting for the telephone to ring exaggerated the oppressive silence in the flat so that it bounced off the walls and closed in all around me.

I picked up the receiver of the telephone to check it was on the hook, then I stood up, walked into the kitchen and made myself a mug of hot Ribena. I walked around a bit, sat down, stood up and then went back to the kitchen and took a few plates out of the cold dirty water in the sink. Why hadn't he telephoned back? I decided to count to five hundred in fives, like the girl in the Dorothy Parker short story. I got to fifty-five.

'Nev . . . '

'Yeh.'

'Look Nev, shall we meet?'

'I'll call you later,' he said. 'There's someone at

186

the door.'

Damn him.

April 15th

Giancarlo left me last night. Yesterday afternoon, when the silence in the flat had wrapped itself around me so that I could hardly breathe, the telephone rang. It was my friend Andy Denny who arrived in London from New York yesterday. He left England three years ago, bankrupt and blue, and now he's a successful business man, having set up a company, buying art for corporations.

We met in the Brasserie, opposite the Conran shop, and giggled about the silly times we used to have with Beatrice, particularly one holiday when the three of us laughed non-stop in Italy. Andy banned topless sun-bathing so Beatrice and I took our tops off at every opportunity, in restaurants, in the river and in his bedroom. He would feign melodramatic disgust. We laughed hysterically for three days until my gut hurt.

'So how is Beatrice?' he asked. 'I tried to telephone her, but her flatmate said she was away.'

'Away where?' It was the first time in years that I haven't known of Beatrice's whereabouts.

'I don't know. I thought you would.'

'We've fallen out.'

'*Oh* yeh,' he said. 'Why?'

I told him the story. Of course he thinks we're mad. 'You can't possibly fall out because of a notebook.'

'We have,' I said, laughing. 'We've split up.'

'Don't be ridiculous,' he said. 'You've got to get back together.'

187

It was late when I got home. GC was in a cold, weird mood and there were a couple of his suitcases by the front door.

'What's the matter?' I asked him.

'That character Nev telephoned twice and left a message to say he can't make it tonight.'

'I don't know what he's talking about,' I said. 'I never arranged to meet him.'

'I don't believe you. You are lying.'

'I'm not,' I screamed.

'And I found a banana skin on the bedside table. The bed not made. We must have a serious talk.'

'What about?' I asked, shivering inside.

'I went to the Portobello Hotel, to find out why the bill was so expensive,' he said. 'You stayed in room 22, a room with a double bed and the management say you were with a man. The man made three telephone calls to a company, Madco, and a couple of long calls to the States. He ordered nine glasses of Double Black Label, no ice, and three bottles of vintage champagne. He also had his jacket and trousers express dry-cleaned and his shirt laundered. He signed a few of the bills. Tracey discovered that Madco is a company that Neville is involved with. What can you say?'

'Giancarlo, it's not what you think. I don't know why you and that maddening Tracey had to snoop around and find out things you don't need to know. Giancarlo, you will have to believe me. Nothing happened between us. Really. You just have to believe me.'

'I cannot. I no longer believe anything you say. I am going back to New York and my solicitor will

188

arrange a legal separation. Anna, why? If you hadn't arranged to see Neville tonight, I don't think I would have brought this matter up. You are a silly girl. Now I must go. Goodbye.'

'Giancarlo, don't go,' I called after him. 'Giancarlo,' I sobbed, 'please don't go.' He was walking down the stairs. 'GIANCARLO, COME BACK,' I shouted. I heard the front door slam. I ran after him in my bare feet. I ran out into the street and saw him getting into a taxi. I raced after the cab waving and shouting. 'GIANCARLO,' I screamed. 'Giancarlo,' I whispered to myself as I sat down on the curb and wept.

I asked a man who was sweeping the road for a cigarette and he rolled me one. I sat there for a while, smoking and blowing circles. It would be all right, I thought, if I could convince Giancarlo that Nev and I have never slept together. Everything would be all right in the end. It had to be. But when I got back to the house, the front door to the building had closed, even though I had wedged the doormat in it. It was a bad sign. I had to ring Ivan's bell because everybody else was out.

'Locked out again?' came his familiar slightly nasal tone through the intercom. 'Was it you screaming downstairs?'

'No,' I said, cursing him under my breath.

I had a sleepless night, tossing and turning from one side to the other. I have smoked a thousand and one cigarettes. The flat is still a bomb-site. Maria comes back tomorrow.

April 16th

Another sleepless night. I tried to telephone GC at his apartment in New York, but the answering machine is on twenty-four hours a day. I called him this morning at work, but brain-dead Tracey said he was in a meeting. 'God,' I said, 'but I would like to speak to him urgently.'

'I'll like get him to call you.'

He never did.

I had lunch with Sapphire. She was sweet and sympathetic. She thinks Giancarlo will come round in the end, but she says it will take a long time. I'm not so sure. We talked it all through and she implied that perhaps I would be better off without him. 'You're not really happy with him,' she said. 'Are you?'

'I am. Oh, I don't know. I feel unsafe without him.'

'Do something for yourself,' she said. 'Carry on with that story you are writing. Perhaps I can show it to someone. Go and see a counsellor. I have the name of somebody who's very good.'

'Who?'

'A woman. I've been seeing her,' she said, 'since I split with John.'

She gave me this woman's number and the name of a book to buy. It's a book about why we all go for the people we do. It seems so tiresome, reading books and going to see shrinks. We can all find out the reasons why we behave like we do, but how can we change old behaviour patterns? How can we actually rid ourselves of the demons that lurk inside?

April 23rd

The last few days have been hell. I wake with a bruised, uneasy heart and for a moment can't think what is wrong – but before too long it all flutters into focus. I have been desperately trying to get through to Giancarlo but his moronic secretary fields my calls with earnest excuses, ranging from, 'He's out of town thru Tuesday playing golf,' to 'He's in the bathroom dabbing some coffee off his tie.'

She has been so diligent and dedicated about protecting him from me and so righteous in her tone, that it makes me suspect that they are having an affair – a sordid, silly, damp little affair. A comic-book affair: the red-nailed, stud-ear-ringed, small-brained secretary and the chic-smelling, richly-tanned boss.

It seems so ironic that my marriage to Giancarlo has folded because of Nev, *because of Nev*, when absolutely nothing flagrant has happened. We haven't even kissed. Our tongues have never touched. Nev with his twisted mouth, dog-bitten nose, unruly, straw-hair and all those moths floating around, nesting in his clothes. Nerdy Nev – winding me up like a clock. If he hadn't been so idiotically indiscreet and left a message with Giancarlo on that fateful night I'm sure GC and I would still be together.

Andy Denny came over a couple of nights ago, to say goodbye. I was in such a perturbed and strange state that I asked him if he wanted to have an affair with me. It seemed like a good idea at the time: he's reasonably attractive and I've known him for ever. We have mutual friends, we make each other laugh and we both love mushroom risotto. Not that I have ever contemplated having an affair with him before, but as I said, I was feeling strange.

Andy laughed and said I must be feeling really traumatised to consider having an affair with him. We both laughed. It did seem a bit desperate. The only light in this tunnel of gloom is that I have made up with Beatrice. Andy had a drink with her and they discussed my decline and fall. She had already heard from Sapphire but Andy urged her to call me to kiss and make up. She telephoned late last night and after some unnatural small talk we managed to laugh about the notebook affair and about my proposition to Andy.

But she bitched about Sapphire. She said Sapphire hardly ever telephones her anymore. 'Sapphire is really serious about her work,' I said. 'She doesn't answer her telephone, she very rarely rings me.'

'But why doesn't she get an answering machine?' Beatrice said in a taut tone. 'Everyone else has one.'

April 25th

I tried to write a bit of the Pig story last night, but I was too distracted and disturbed. I just sat, staring at the icy white page, wondering how to crack it and what to do with my life and then I thought of Nick and I dialled his number and astonishingly he answered. He'd only been back from Arizona,

192

where he was filming the Levi's ad, for a couple of hours, so me telephoning at that moment was quite cute and telepathic. We had a long conversation and then decided to meet in a Thai restaurant in South Kensington.

He's so young and fresh after Nev-Moth. He's going to be a star, a blue-eyed boy, courted far and wide and worshipped by triangular-breasted schoolgirls. He's just been cast in a new Scorsese film with Brad Pitt, Hugh Grant and Juliette Lewis. Nick plays Juliette Lewis' weird and obsessive ex-boyfriend who stalks her across America and then to France, befriends her lovers and draws them away from her. He's obviously blissed-out to get the part and sparks of energy danced between us charging the evening with glamour and importance and anticipation of exciting things about to happen.

It was great to see him. It's not exactly that I missed Nick while he was away, but perhaps that was because there was so many dramas going on in my life. We talked, but it was really me who talked. As usual he gave very little away. I suspect that he has at least two or three girlfriends. He kind of admits to the one in Paris, although when I mentioned her last night, he claimed that it was over and that she had never meant that much to him. He said that sleeping with her had been a kind of sexual addiction.

He asked if he could come home with me.

Tomorrow he's leaving for sixteen weeks to film with Scorsese. First he goes to San Francisco and then Paris. He said it would be our last chance to be together and all that la di da stuff, but he didn't really urge me and I didn't feel he was offering anything more than what he could give me there and then, at that moment, for those few hours. And I am really not ready for a sexual encounter, particularly not in the marital bed, and it's difficult to just curl-up with Nick.

When I left him late and went home, I was feeling acutely lonely and in need of a chat. Maria was up making coffee, but she was only vaguely sympathetic. She said, 'Oh poor you,' but then she insinuated that if I was feeling lonely I only had myself to blame. She's obviously taken Giancarlo's side. She said, 'I told you that man Nev was bad. I tell you and you never listen to me.' Smug old cow. Smelly SOC. She's not really a girl's girl. She's an eyelashing, lip-pouting, breast-thrusting, hair-flicking flirt.

I miss Giancarlo. The world feels like a very big place without him. He hasn't returned my calls, my many messages pleading with him to ring me.

April 29th

That hypocritical hussy-harlot Maria. I overheard her on the telephone with Nev. I heard her say that I didn't want to talk to him, but then she started giggling and saucing and sexing him up in that husky Spanish voice.

I confronted her, but she looked wide-eyed and flushed and she said I was imagining things.

April 30th

Today I received a sweet letter from Giancarlo that made me feel sad –

Dear Anna,

It is best for both of us that we do not speak or see each other at the moment, so please don't keep telephoning my office and leaving messages on the machine at home. Of course I am not having an affair with Tracey. The idea is mad.

Please understand, our marriage has finished. It is over. It is not easy for me to say this, but I thought about it carefully and this is the only course of action left open to me. We have had good times together and you have made me very happy. You are funny and charming and sweet. I have loved you very much and probably still do. It is not just the question of if you or if you have not slept with another man, (although of course I don't like the idea that you have). It is because I no longer trust you. Lying is a disaster for marriage, or for any relationship.

You are very vulnerable, like a child who needs much care and love and attention. Knowing this, I tried to love you very much, perhaps too much and I tried to take care of you. You will do great things with your life if only you can believe in yourself. Maybe you are not yet ready.

195

Perhaps you need time alone. One day you will love yourself a little more and then you will be happy to love a man who really cares for you, as I do.

I am not perfect. I have probably spent rather too much time thinking of business. You are always laughing at me and telling me I can't relax. You say I am hiding from myself. We shall see. But now you must let me go as I must let you go.

Good things will happen to you and I will be so proud . . .

. . . Oh God, it breaks my heart. As Doug would say, 'It's all so real.' Giancarlo is right. It is naïve of me to blame everything on Nev, to say that if he had not done xyz, abc would not have happened. I let it happen. I did not behave in an honourable way. What's happened has happened for a reason. I do need time on my own. I have been with some kind of a boyfriend since the age of sixteen. In a strange way his letter is a relief. He's made a decision and there is nothing I can do to alter it. And he does not hate me, that is something at least.

May 1st

I'm in Gloucestershire with May. Yesterday evening as a grim Sunday was drawing to its nadir, with the start of those religious programmes on television, I suddenly realised that it was a Bank Holiday weekend. I had been wondering why no one appeared to be around apart from Matthew Clivesmith who hates Sundays, bank holidays, Christmas and Easter and never makes any effort to do anything special for them. I was missing Giancarlo. I even missed the way he nags me to tidy up and make the bed. I spent the whole day writing drafts of a letter to him and then scrunching up pieces of paper and throwing them on the ground. It was really quite late when I packed a small bag and caught the last train to Stroud.

It's lovely to be here, although May is worried because her hands are painfully arthritic and she says she can't drive herself around any more, which makes her feel helpless and marooned. She's been lovely as always, very supportive and encouraging. She says she never thought Giancarlo was right for me: she thinks he is too much of a perfectionist and repressed in some way. 'You haven't met the love of your life yet, darling,' she said, which cheered me up.

It was two months since Geraldine had started work for Rory Gunn Ltd. She was rarely at work before nine forty-five. Her clothes always looked dishevelled and un-ironed and her appearance, generally, was unkempt. Rabbit noticed and said something to Badger about it. Badger was already concerned about her time-keeping – she usually took an hour and a half for lunch instead of an hour. She also made far too many private telephone calls. He asked Pig to have a word with her.

'GGGeraldine,' Pig stammered, 'we don't think it's appropriate for you to make so many private telephone calls during office hours.'

'I'm sorry,' she said tearfully, 'I'm looking for somewhere to live.'

'You don't have anywhere to live?'

'Well, yes, not exactly. I mean I do, but I'm unhappy. I need to move out, it's not going well.' She began to cry and she leant forward and put her head in her arms. Pig put his hands on her shoulders. She lifted her head and wiped away the tears. Pig gave her a handkerchief, and decided that he would tell his father that Geraldine had personal problems and that they would have to treat her kindly. 'Thank you,' she said, blowing her nose.

The following afternoon Pig stood by Geraldine's desk waiting for her to get off the telephone. She made a sign to Pig, circling her arm to indicate that whoever it was would not get off the line. Pig waited patiently. Geraldine laughed. 'I've got to go,' she said, and then she laughed again and flicked some ash from her cigarette into a small ashtray. 'I'll see you,' she said, 'eight o'clock. Bye. Me too.'

'Sorry,' she said to Pig, 'that was my mother. I couldn't get her to stop talking.'

'BBBBadger wants to see you.'

'Right,' said Geraldine, stubbing out her cigarette.

Pig sat at the reception desk. He put all the paper clips back in their box, filled the stapler with a new packet of staples and threw away several scrunched-up pieces of paper. He sat up, looked around, leant down and retrieved one of the scrunched-up balls from the waste-paper basket. He opened it up, it was half a letter written in Geraldine's hand:

Darling,

I do love you. I do care, I really do. I don't
want it all to end. Please believe me, nothing
happened with that man, nothing at all. We
never even kissed. Could we not meet, some
time soon . . . ?

The door was opening, Pig crushed the paper in
his hand and threw it back in the bin. 'Wwhat did
he say?' Pig asked.

'It's great,' Geraldine said, clapping her hands together. 'Really great. He's giving me some extra
money to buy clothes.' But Pig noticed that when
her smile faded, she looked strained and very tired.
How he longed to put his arms around her, stroke
her forehead and soothe her.

Pig imagined that the man she had written the
note to was not treating her in the right way. She
was obviously far too good for him. He made her
unhappy. Maybe it was he, Pig, she was referring
to in the note. He was *that* man that nothing had
happened with. The letter was probably to that
arrogant conceited chap Peter, who suspected him,
Pig, of being her suitor, that was the reason he was
a bit off with him on the telephone. If that was the
case, he would have to take extra special care of
Geraldine and make sure she really was all right.

A couple of weeks later Geraldine still looked a
mess, despite Badger's extra money, and she was
moody. Sometimes she typed the letters she was
given, spoke good French to the clients and laughed
with Pig, but at other times she would say very little
and she would find errands to do outside the office.

199

On the down days she sat at her desk but she was very detached, hardly there at all. She would sit, staring into space and smoking cigarettes, glancing at her watch and she wouldn't smile when Pig attempted to make a joke.

May 3rd

When I returned to the flat last night, I found Nev drinking a bottle of wine with Maria. Maria stood up, picked up an ashtray full of butt-ends and an empty bottle of wine and disappeared.

'Oh there you are,' Nev said. 'I've been waiting for you to get back.'

'What do you want?' I asked him. 'What are you doing here?'

'Like I said, waiting for you.'

'Like hell.'

'I promise you,' he said. 'Ask Maria.'

'Sure,' I said, lighting a cigarette. 'She's much too busy flirting to remember that perhaps it is me who you came to see.'

'Look,' he said, 'darling, of course it's you I came to see. I heard about you and Giancarlo.'

'Who from?'

'I can't remember, but it's wonderful news,' he said. 'Why don't we buy some bottles of champagne and go back to my house and *celebrate*.' He jumped up, then came over and hugged me hard and lifted me off the ground. I struggled and asked him to put me down.

'It's because you so tactlessly informed Giancarlo that you couldn't meet me the other night that he decided to leave me,' I said.

200

'What night? I don't know what you are talking about,' he said. 'I haven't spoken to Giancarlo.'

'I don't believe you.'

He shrugged. 'Don't you see,' he said. 'He was testing you.'

'So you're saying that the last time we spoke and you said you would get back to me, you never did. You never telephoned and left a message with Giancarlo to say you couldn't meet me. Now that is appalling behaviour.'

'No I didn't telephone,' he said. 'I was stuck in the dark-room, but I have been trying to call you for the last week or so.'

'What do you do in the dark-room?' I asked. 'Find yourself? You'll be in there for the rest of your life. And where the hell are my wedding photographs?'

'I think of you in the dark room,' he said, taking my hand.

'I've been looking at the photographs of the wedding day, there is a strange aura around you and Giancarlo. The marriage obviously wasn't meant to be. I've got the contacts at my flat. Why don't we go back there and you can see what I mean?'

'I'm not sure,' I said.

'Come on,' he said, taking my hand again and squeezing the last bit of resistance from me. 'Come on, darling.'

I thought, why not? Just go to the flat, look at the photographs, check out the aura, have a drink and see how it goes. Then, just as we were leaving, he told me to wait by the door. He said he'd forgotten something. He slunk off and I heard him chatting with Maria. I heard her laugh.

201

'Why did you do that?' I asked when he got back.
'Do what?'
'Have an intimate goodbye chat with Maria.'
'Oh come on,' he said. 'Get a grip.'
We bought five bottles of champagne at the off-licence and a packet of balloons, that had probably been left over from Christmas and were slashed down in price. His flat was perfectly tidy; there was a vase of yellow roses on the table, the bed was made, the washing-up washed up, but the glass in the window panes was cracked, the cream bed cover was frayed and there was a saucepan on the ring half-filled with congealing rice.

He blew up the balloons and tied them to the wooden chairs, where they hung rather forlornly like decaying tulips. A long string of delicate beads made from burnt-red coloured seeds, that he had once brought back from India, was draped over one of the bed knobs. He gave them to me. But I wondered how many strings of those beads he had bargained for under the hot Indian sun. How many girls had he strung along?

He put the first champagne bottle between his legs and pulled out the cork. He poured me a glass in a dark blue flute that he had probably found in the Portobello Market. He played a song called 'Too Cool to Drool' over and over again. It's a great song, funky and soulful and he pulled me up off my chair and we danced to it. He's a wooden dancer, he dances a bit like a Thunderbird puppet. Later he found a blank tape and recorded 'Too Cool to Drool' six times in a row, and then he rummaged in a drawer and pulled out a post card of a pair of Spanish flamenco dancers:
202

a drawing of a dark man wearing a red shirt with white polka dots, black trousers piped in white and red cowboy boots and a girl in a red dress with real material stuck on the skirt. He scribbled To Anna, love always, Nev, on the back and handed me the tape.

Another bottle was opened, champagne foam spraying everywhere. Nev sat down, then stood up again and went to a shelf and pulled down a yellow box stuffed full of contacts from the wedding which I studied through a magnifying glass. He's right. In one or two photographs of Giancarlo and me there is an eerie whitish shimmer around us, not visible without the magnifying glass.

Nev opened the third bottle and drank most of it himself. The song 'Too Cool to Drool' was beginning to drive me a little crazy, the drum-beat was drumming in my head, and looking at the wedding photographs had made me feel a bit low. I was dancing, but with no zest and I was thinking about going home and crashing out.

Nev opened the fourth bottle and took a great gulp, foam and drink oozed on to his face and dribbled down his neck. He wiped his hands on his jeans and then took another long gulp and handed the bottle to me. I gave it back to him. Half an hour later he passed out on the bed. He was like dead lead and I couldn't move him or wake him. He was snoring like a dog and his flies were undone. He looked third-hand, worn-out and done-in. I took off his shoes and covered him with a duvet. I knew then that the moment had definitely passed, the moment between Nev and me was never going to be.

May 4th

After leaving Nev, I went home and read the book that Sapphire recommended. It's called *Healthy Love* and is all about why people pursue sick relationships with each other. It's completely riveting, like looking at photographs of oneself. I am a classic: 'love addicts' are attracted to people who are terrified of being hooked-up in a relationship. The book describes those people as 'avoidance addicts'.

Of course I have all the love addict symptoms and all my boyfriends bar Giancarlo are Avoidance Addicts. *Healthy Love* says that 'love addicts' have a terrible fear of being abandoned but an underlying fear of intimacy and were usually abandoned physically or emotionally by their parents when they were children.

It's true that I feel more attracted to a man who is fairly ambiguous about his affection for me. So when someone like Giancarlo pops up begging me to marry him and making desperate declarations of love, I run because it feels unfamiliar and almost distasteful.

Men like Nev and Doug were controlled by somebody else's neediness when they were children, the book says, and are terrified of becoming involved in an intimate relationship, but to complicate matters they also have an underlying fear of being abandoned. So we kick in together and play off each other. The affair between a love addict and an avoidance addict feels passionate and obsessive when in fact it is very sick.

I read until four this morning and when I woke at eleven, I telephoned Nev and announced that I wouldn't be able to see him any more. He said, 'OK, fine,' in an off-hand manner and then asked me why I was being so dramatic. I didn't tell him that I was exasperated by his petty, schoolboy games, and that I no longer found his bitten nose and dribbling mouth attractive. God. How could I have contemplated sleeping with him? I told him about the book and suggested that he read it, and of course he scoffed and laughed and said something like, 'Oh you're such a sucker for all that American psycho-babble, but then you would be.'

I laughed too and wished I hadn't.

I'm in a Piggish mood. I may even finish today.

Geraldine had been with the Gunns for six months, when, at the end of a hot July, she gave in her notice. She told Badger that she needed to find a job which paid a higher salary. Pig had noticed that in the last few weeks money had regularly gone missing from the petty cash box. He was pretty sure that Geraldine had been taking it, but he decided not to tell his father.

Badger wasn't sorry about the idea of losing Geraldine, although he knew his son had a soft spot for the girl, so he kept his thoughts to himself. Pig was numbed with pain and despair and he didn't say a word on the train home that evening. He hadn't spoken to anyone since Geraldine had told him the news of her imminent departure at lunch time. After supper that night, Pig went straight to bed. He spent most of the weekend upstairs in his bedroom, and on Monday morning he said he wasn't feeling well, so Badger took the train to London alone.

When Badger returned that evening, he delivered two cards to Pig. One was from Piglet and one from Geraldine. Piglet's was a jokey card. Inside she'd written, 'Do get well, Piggy. Masses of love from Piglet.' Geraldine had sent a post card, a still-life of some pears and a pot of flowers by Cézanne. On the back she had written, 'Sorry to hear you are off your food, hope you are back at the trough soon! Love Geraldine.'

He smiled at the Piggy reference and the jokey exclamation mark and he obsessed about the use of the word 'Love'. She could have written 'Best Wishes', or 'Regards', but she had chosen to write 'Love'. There must be a reason for that. A good reason. He kept the card close to him and picked it up and looked at it several times that evening. He almost rang her at home, to thank her for the card, but thought better of it.

Rabbit came up to Pig's room with a bowl of chicken soup on a tray. He showed her Geraldine's card and then asked her to persuade his father to offer Geraldine a pay-rise. She promised to have a word. She would try anything to get Pig back to his old, piggy, self. Rabbit was quite fond of Geraldine. She was a beautiful girl, although she didn't make the best of herself. She looked rather wan and undernourished.

'I really think,' Rabbit said to Badger in a formidable tone, 'that it would be preferable to offer

Geraldine a pay-rise rather than pay a huge commission to an agency and go through the tiresome chore of finding a new girl.' Badger suspected that his wife was coercing him to offer Geraldine a pay-rise for Pig's sake. However he did not like to quarrel with his wife, she was a small woman, but an awesome one.

May 6th

Lunch with Dad today. He says he feels broke so we went to Pizza Express near the Kensington Odeon. A waitress in a red and black uniform was irritatingly enthusiastic when we walked through the door, and she showed us to a table topped with two sad pink and white bud carnations in a small white vase, destined never to bloom. The pizzas came alarmingly quickly, so we sat for a long time after we had finished eating, drinking. I was drinking warm Diet Coke, but Dad was drinking glasses of red wine. He likes to order glasses rather than a bottle because it makes him feel he is drinking less.

Dad asked me about Giancarlo but I didn't really want to discuss it with him – he's not very good on emotional issues – so I changed the subject and asked him how he was. He says his doctor has advised him to stop drinking because his liver is very weak, but like a fool he says he can't imagine life without drink. He says drink is really more important to him than life. It couldn't be more depressing.

'You could always go to AA. Alcoholics Anonymous. Eric Clapton goes. It really works, Dad. Why don't you give it a go?' I said.

That remark spun him off into a diatribe: 'Do you really imagine that I'm going to sit in a cosy circle along with a whole load of raddled ex-alkies in a drafty

208

church hall or community centre, listening to a sad
and sorry soul sharing the story of his drinking days.
Listen to him gravely telling us about the beatings he
gave his wife and the way he ignored his children, but,
hey, life is much better now he's discovered sobriety,
the programme, the twelve steps. Think again, girl.
Not me. No, I'd rather drown in a vat of whisky.

'The boredom. The boredom of sitting there listening to those pathetic life stories while sipping
tepid tea or instant coffee out of plastic cups. It's so
undignified. "Hello I'm Richard and I'm an alcoholic.
I'm powerless over my addiction." (He mimicked in
an American accent.)

'I can't stand all that sharing and caring, and holding
hands while saying some kind of prayer. Serenity, I
think they call it. Moony stuff. And then when the
meeting is over there is always the terrible, horrifying,
fear that some clean and serene woman will come
over and hug you or one of the men will warmly
shake your hand. Ugh. I admit I *am* powerless over
my addiction, but I enjoy it. I like to drink. Drinking
suits me.'

I studied his familiar face, once handsome and
hopeful, but now resigned and worn, lined like an
old man's palm. His pale, blue eyes are growing
smaller and weaker and puffier by the day, his mop
of thick, white hair is coarse, the jowly cheeks flaccid
and bloodshot and the thin lips stained dark red from
the wine. It would take years to change his view and
perhaps he has chosen his own sort of euthanasia. It
is a sad but true fact that there is nothing I can do. I
was amazed, though, that he knew so much about
the meetings.

'Dad. Wow. How do you know so much about it?' I asked.

'I went twice.'

'So there was a moment when you wanted to give up?'

'Dr Levinson pushed me. He said my liver was burning out and he strongly advised me to give up and to go to a meeting. But after my second meeting I realised I'd rather die pissed a few years earlier than stagger on sober clinging on to a plastic cup of instant coffee. I told Dr Levinson what I thought of his blasted meetings. He smiled and told me it was my life. He never said a truer word.'

It seemed awful that Dad wasn't going to be around much longer and that he didn't appear to care.

'Dad, there are alternative non-alcoholic drinks. You don't have to just drink coffee in a plastic cup. You could drink ginger ale with angastura bitters or V8 juice.'

'V8? What's that? A vitamin drink?' He spat out the word vitamin with venom.

'It's delicious,' I said, feeling more and more like a hearty girl guide. 'It's a mixed vegetable juice made from carrots, celery, beetroot, parsley, lettuce, watercress and spinach, and it's only sixty calories.'

'How disgusting,' Dad said. 'And why are you, a shadow of a girl, worried about calories.'

'Oh, Dad, for God's sake it's just a healthy and rather delicious drink which happens not to be as fattening as a banana milkshake.'

'Healthy. It may be healthy today, but in ten years' time some clever dick with a bow tie will declare that carrots cause cancer of the cervix, just you wait and see. I've been allergic to vegetables since we were forced to eat over-cooked cabbage at school. No, real men don't drink celery juice.'

I sighed loudly, defeated and exhausted by him.

'But your mother, Stella,' he went on, 'now she loves all this meeting stuff.'

'Does she?' I asked. 'I had no idea. What, AA meetings?'

'No, no, no, something else, some other meeting meant for families and friends of alcoholics and druggies. I told her about my talk with Dr Levinson and she went to see him herself, and he pointed her in the general direction. The rest she did herself. She's been going for quite a few weeks now. Why don't you discuss it all with her? She said she hadn't heard from you in a long time.'

'I haven't heard from her.'

'I don't think she thinks you want to hear from her. I think she's ashamed of her recent behaviour. You should give her a ring.'

'Thanks for the tip, Dad. Maybe I will.' I wanted to say how come you are suddenly so concerned, Dad, you've been ignoring her for years, but I kept quiet.

Just before we left, I asked him about Greg and the restaurant deal. Dad flipped, slagged him off no end and said he was trouble with a capital T. Basically he had wanted Dad to invest all the money in the project, while he sat back organising the list for the opening party. Apparently Greg is bankrupt and owes money everywhere, and will probably be driven out of town. Of course I was delighted and

211

told Dad that I had tried to warn him. I said that Greg would sell his mother to the devil given half the chance. Dad said it didn't matter anyway and then he told me that he is going back to Nassau to start a wholesale swimming suit business with a man called Mario.

'That's certainly different, Dad,' I said. 'That's great.' I picked up his wine glass and slugged back the remains. 'Here's to you.'

'Thank you, darling,' he said summoning the waiter and ordering one last glass.

May 7th

Pig was in the office singing to himself. He was a happy old Pig because Geraldine had accepted the pay-rise. Without his intervention, he mused, she would have left the cosy confines of the office, ousted into the world, broke, alone and sad.

Pig often fantasised about Geraldine.

He fantasised that he had her to himself outside the office. Often they would just go out for dinner and talk. His parents went to the theatre occasionally and there was a theatre trip planned for the following week. Pig fantasised about asking Geraldine to accompany him. He had almost asked her several times, but whenever he had summoned enough courage and was poised to form the words, she had walked away or answered the telephone or rushed out to lunch.

Geraldine was concentrating very hard on tidying her desk. She hadn't spoken to Pig all day, not a word since she had mumbled good morning.

212

'Gggeraldine,' Pig stuttered, 'wwwwould you like to come to the theatre with me next week?'

'What play is it?' she asked, without looking up from her task.

'Ummm, I ccan't remember, but it's on at the National and Maggie Smith is in it. Oh, please come, Geraldine.'

'I don't think I can.' Geraldine was twisting the ring on her middle finger. 'I don't think it's a good idea.'

'Wwwhy not?'

'I just don't. We work together. Don't worry, Roland, you can ask someone else.'

Pig hummed. 'I'm a fat old Pig, jolly old Pig, fat and old and jolly . . .'

'Roland?' Geraldine said.

'Yes?'

'I won't be able to type that report you gave me. I've got an urgent appointment, so I'll have to leave in about ten minutes. OK?'

The OK was a rhetorical question, but Pig felt he must reply.

'Yyyes, of course,' he said.

'And tomorrow. I won't be in all day, I have to recover from my appointment.'

'That's all right,' Pig said. 'Call us tomorrow and let us know how you are getting on.'

'Thanks Pig.' She gave him a small smile. 'I'll try to.'

The End.

May 9th

I telephoned Stella and we arranged to meet for tea in
a café near her house. I was there first, flicking through
an *Evening Standard* and feeling a little apprehensive
because I haven't seen her for such a long time. I was
imagining that perhaps the meetings had transformed
her into a saintly, God-like, humble person and that
we were going to get on really well, but I was slightly
irritated when she spun in twenty minutes late, wearing a wide straw hat, with a pink bow, a long purple
skirt dotted with tiny mirrors and a pair of lime-green
espadrilles.

She kissed me quickly on the cheek and then summoned the waiter and ordered tea. She demanded
that the tea be not too strong, with some hot water
on the side and skimmed milk, no sugar. She then
changed her mind and asked for mineral water with
a piece of lime. Of course they didn't have lime in
the middle of Chelsea, so she settled for lemon and
I watched her and thought my God, I'm in danger of
becoming my mother. That is me there. Capricious
in restaurants. And I made a mental note never to
change my mind when ordering food again.

Apart from the tea incident she wasn't nearly so
selfish and mad as usual, although three quarters of
our meeting was taken up with her talking about
herself. It's true. She is going to meetings. She says
214

it's a miracle to find people like her, who have had the same kind of experience as she has and managed to pull through. The most sane thing she said was that she can't blame everything on Dad. She has now discovered that she has her own problems to sort out.

She confided that a year ago she didn't really see the point of going on, she was terrified of Dad leaving, but was miserable when he was around. But now, since going to the meetings, she has new friends, and feels much more optimistic about life. She seemed concerned that Giancarlo and I have separated. She said, 'He's a good man, believe me, there are not many out there.' And then we talked about me for a whole ten minutes and I savoured every second of it.

Giancarlo is a good man and that is why I do find it difficult to extricate him from my life. Maybe he's right. Maybe I'm not quite ready for all that love and caring and worship. Being with him would have meant that a part of my soul would have died and the awful truth is that he would never have noticed. But I do love him and I don't think anybody has ever loved me quite so much.

May 11th

I had a letter from Giancarlo's solicitor today. He wants a divorce, although he has offered me the flat and he is willing to pay me substantial alimony. He's a generous, wonderful man, although I wish I had the courage to give up this flat, Maria, the whole Giancarlo experience.

Nev telephoned this evening and asked to speak

215

to Maria. I hung up on him. He called back and I shouted out to Maria, 'Maria, it's Nev for you.'

May 13th

I am consumed with worry and fear and I'm shaking all over. May had a heart attack this afternoon while fiddling around in the herb garden and she's collapsed. An ambulance took her to hospital and someone managed to resuscitate her, but apparently she is still quite coma-like, very dehydrated, and not off the critical list. The professor telephoned this morning and warbled the news. Stella and I are on the train now but I couldn't get hold of Sapphire, because she's not answering the telephone, so I had to leave her a dramatic note.

We are here at the hospital. May is in intensive care wired up to terrifying tubes. Stella, the professor and I are hanging around in a poky, smoky little room, which is furnished with three chairs, a two-year-old copy of *Woman's Own* and a drinks machine which makes a brown drink called tea and a brown drink called coffee.

I don't think May really knew who we were, although a whisper of a smile appeared on her lips when Stella and I tip-toed in. The professor hasn't left her side. He's sitting with a droopy face and holding her clammy hand. She looks deathly pale. She is hooked up by tube to one machine in case her heart goes again, and she has a saline drip going into her arm. There is a fearsome, fatal feel around her which makes everything feel cold.

216

May 14th

Sapphire arrived this afternoon by train and took a taxi to the hospital. May is still coma-like, breathing slowly, but it's not the breath of life. We have sat here all deathly-day, watching her in a trance while doctors and nurses rush in and out. Stella broke down in the late afternoon and said she wished it was her who was lying there instead. She went into a morbid monologue about how awful her life was, what was the point of going on and all the old stuff. She then kissed May's forehead and said she had to get back to London and go to a meeting. It's a relief that she's gone because she is not a soothing presence.

Sapphire and I are sitting silently, smoking in the poky, smoky room. We are desperate for her to make it, but I think we both know she won't. 'Do you think she'll come through?' I keep asking.

'Yes,' Sapphire says doubtfully and then a few seconds later she asks me the same question. The professor left for a good deal of the day and has just returned in a maudlin state. He says he has never loved somebody so much. Nor have I.

May 16th

She died this morning.

I was in the loo at the actual time of her death.

We are all back at Waterford, sitting huddled in the corner of the drawing room, drinking tea. I am quite

217

calm, numbed probably, with shock. We have been telephoning people to let them know. Sapphire broke the news to her brother, Roddy, and I have spoken to May's closest friends: Alice, Anthea and Lee. Stella telephoned Dad in Nassau and he's coming back for the funeral.

Everyone is devastated by the suddenness of her death. One of the young doctors said that it was no good thing that May smoked very heavily. I have been chain-smoking all day. I feel sad, mad and empty. This large house is so cold without her, cold and soulless. Stella returned from London late this morning. She rushed up to me and said we needed to talk, then she collapsed in a chair and sobbed.

I telephoned Giancarlo ten minutes ago at home and told him the news. He was sympathetic but he sounded preoccupied as if he was with somebody.

May 17th

I woke in the night convinced that May was in the room. I could smell her lavender eau de cologne and her jack russell, Daisy, who was sleeping on my bed woke up and then whimpered and wagged her tail. She never actually appeared in ghost-form. Thank God. I was afraid she would be a pale and clammy apparition, like she was at her death. I didn't breath, and I begged her to leave. After her presence evaporated, I was lulled back to sleep, and I slept deeply and well.

May is going to be cremated and the ashes spread in the rose garden. She always said she wanted to be cremated rather than buried. She didn't want her

218

body to rot away underground. She said the idea made her feel claustrophobic. We are having a small family funeral and then perhaps we will arrange a memorial later on.

Beatrice telephoned and after a session commiserating she gleefully told me that she had bumped into Nev and *Maria* last night. She saw them together at a pub called the Westbourne in Notting Hill. Of course this information irked me, and perhaps I over-reacted. I shouted at Beatrice and asked her why she had to tell me, and she said she had no idea that I would be so upset. I shouted that I wasn't upset, and then I hung up. I have decided to telephone Giancarlo and tell him to give Maria her notice.

Sapphire says I can't possibly think about Maria and Nev at a time like this.

May 18th

I telephoned Giancarlo late last night and we chatted about May and then I said I couldn't cope with Maria or anyone else in the house when I return to London. He said he understood and that he would write, giving her one month's notice. But then he blew me right away. He said he was seeing Head of a Cow, that Spanish bitch we saw in Spain, and he wanted me to know before I heard it from anyone else.

'Great, Giancarlo,' I said, falsely bright. 'I'm very happy for you.'

When I had put the telephone down, I sat for a long time in an armchair in May's yellow study, staring out of the window at the dark, starless sky.

May 19th

I am so overtired that I am unable to sleep. I was awake all night thinking about everything, particularly the staggering way Giancarlo has forgotten me so easily. I knew something was up in Madrid when that bitch Head of a Cow had her hand on his knee. I telephoned him this morning in New York and burst into tears. 'How could you?' I asked. 'How could you go off with Cora so quickly? Why do you want to be with someone else now when all this is going on?'

'I am sorry,' he said. 'I cannot arrange my love life around the births and deaths of your family.'

'Giancarlo,' I blurted out, 'that is a horrible thing to say.'

'I'm sorry,' he said again. 'What I said is not in good taste, but it is better that you hear from me, rather than someone else.'

'But, Giancarlo, I do love you ... I've always loved you. It's just ...'

'I love you too, but we are no longer married,' he said, quite blunt and cold and final.

May 21st

Yesterday afternoon just before we all left, a man called Mr Asquith telephoned from May's solicitor's office and asked to speak to Mrs Hunt's daughter. 'There's been a mistake,' I said, 'I'm Anna Blaker, her niece, but there are no daughters or any sons for that matter.'

He coughed and then mumbled a brief apology.

*

When I got back to London, the flat was still and quiet, and there was no answer when I knocked on Maria's bedroom door. I crept in and was confronted with the sight of Nev's hand-knit orange sweater on her bed, an empty packet of ten Benson and Hedges cigarettes on the floor, and a purple lacy bra hanging over the chair. The evidence of them being together right there, right here twisted my gut.

I imagined them snooping around my bedroom and reading my letter from Giancarlo and then I had a vision of Maria trying on my clothes, parading up and down for Nev, perhaps doing a silly striptease. The thought of him massaging her, crushing her and hugging her like he had massaged, hugged and crushed me in the past freaked me out. I thought of him kissing her and fondling her breasts. He has never kissed me and there was a point when I desperately wanted him to, but he wouldn't because he is a master of the Mechanics of Desire.

I became more and more incensed until I was almost at a point of raving hysteria. I knew I had to take a few deep breaths and calm myself down. I picked up *Healthy Love*, but its unromantic, generalised and anaesthetised message irritated me. I know that Nev is a gutless, fucked-up avoidance addict but attraction just ain't a sensible thing. At least he's an original and there seem to be fewer and fewer of those types around. Of course I did sabotage my marriage by playing around with him, but my marriage was not meant to be, and I obviously wasn't happy or I wouldn't have gone for a moth-man.

I waited for Maria to get home, and when at last

she did, I sat in my room until she called my name and knocked at the door. I had imagined hurling abuse at her, or throwing something but when it came to it I just sat at the edge of the bed and she stood rather sombrely in the doorway and said how sorry she was to hear about May.

I thanked her and as she turned to leave, I called her back. I wanted to say, how could you carouse around with Nev, how dare you? Don't you realise he's using you to get at me? But I managed to keep calm and I told her that I wanted some time on my own and it was quite likely that I would want to move from the flat so it would be a good idea if she started to look around for another job. She took it quite well, and said she would ask a few friends and then, as she was going through the door, I couldn't resist saying, 'Maybe Nev could find you something,' just so she knew I knew. She turned back with a grimace and said, 'Nev, bah, what a loser, what a silly man, he can't find his way through the door.' Layers of discomfort fell off me and I laughed, laughter of relief.

May 23rd

I am confused and mad with fear. Dad flew back from Nassau yesterday and we had a distressing dinner last night. He said how sorry he was to hear about my disintegrating marriage and how upset he was that May had died. We talked for a long time about May and how wonderful she was and Dad said what superb taste she had and then towards the end of a rather sober dinner, I told him about Mr Asquith, the solicitor, telephoning and asking to speak to May's daughter.

222

'It was strange,' I said, 'to come out with something like that.'

'Have you told Stella?' Dad asked.

'No, why?'

'There is something we have to discuss with you. We've been meaning to tell you . . .'

'What?'

'It's a bit of a mess, Annie,' he said and he suddenly looked tired and his eyelids were heavy and he was fiddling with his tie.

A tight drum was beating inside. Dad was taking an age to light his cigarette. 'What Dad? Stella has been trying to tell me something but she hasn't got round to it. What the hell is going on? Tell me.' I knew then that he was going to tell me something life-changing, something big and bad and dangerous to know and I think I even knew what he was going to say before he said it.

'I will tell you,' he said looking me in the eye, taking my hand, 'May . . . May is not your aunt. May is your mother.'

'May is my *mother*?' My crisp matter-of-fact tone surprised me. 'So who is Stella?'

'Stella is your aunt.'

'Jesus. What do you mean?' I said, knowing exactly what he meant and now knowing why Stella has always been so difficult. It's because I'm not her daughter. Dad had finished one glass of wine and had started on another.

'Your mother . . . Stella and I adopted you because May was unable to cope. She had an affair with a married man, a man she was passionately in love with, a man I think she would have died for. But

223

this man, Rupert Holliwell, had a neurotic wife who threatened to commit suicide if he left her. He was plagued with guilt and not prepared to take that risk.

May was forty-five when you were born, she really wanted a baby, because she knew it was her last chance, but when it actually came down to it, when she realised that this man was not going to leave his wife, despite the fact that she had given birth to his child, she collapsed in depression. She just couldn't cope with the idea of bringing you up on her own. Rupert Holliwell is now dead, he would be about eighty if he were alive. I only met him once. He was an attractive man, tall and dry. He played the piano very well.'

'What did he do?' I asked.

'He managed his estate. Waterstone House was a house he inherited from his mother and gave to May.'

'Oh my God,' I said, 'so there is a man out there somewhere, a man of about *sixty* who is my half-brother. The man who started the law-suit to claim Waterstone.'

'Don't worry about him,' Dad said, smiling. 'That is the least of your problems at the moment.'

'Yes,' I said, looking down at my bowl and watching a tear dripping into my gazpacho. 'But Dad, how could she give me away like that?'

'She was a basket case for six years after you were born,' Dad said. 'She lay in her bedroom, watching the wallpaper, she hardly read a book. Mrs Mason was employed full-time to look after her, to bring her trays of food and help her into the bath. By the time she had recovered you were six years old. It would

224

have been far too traumatic for you to go back to her and anyway we didn't want you to.'

'It's pretty traumatic now,' I said. 'It's all so clear now, my problem with Stella. I wish someone had told me. It would have made life much easier to deal with.'

'May was too ashamed to tell you the truth. It was always understood that you were not to know.'

'May was wrong. I should have been told. Dad, you're not even my father. I just can't believe it,' I said, wiping my eyes with a napkin.

'I love you like a daughter, darling.'

At that moment Dad summoned the waiter and broke his no spirit resolution by ordering a double whisky, no ice. 'As far as I am concerned you are my daughter. We never had any other children. Maybe it was meant to be like this.'

We sat in silence for a while. I smoked a cigarette, Dad finished his whisky and then wrote something invisible in the air with his hand to summon the bill. The bill arrived and Dad handed the man a credit card, which was brought back moments later, unable to be used. When it was time to leave he gave me a hug and whispered, 'It's all right, darling,' in my ear. I don't think we said much more. What more could be said?

May 25th

I have been feeling perplexed and disorientated since the revelation. And there are so many unanswered questions:

What did my father, Rupert Holliwell, look like? And what was his star-sign? Did he ever see me?

225

Did May send him photographs? Did he like to watch bull-fights or did he think it was a cruel sport? Was he romantic? What kind of books did he read? Stella only met him twice and said that he was very attractive, quiet and intelligent.

I am deeply disillusioned that the woman I worshipped, my mother, gave me away, lent me out to her sister. It's so shocking that my parents are not my parents. That Stella is my aunt, that Dad is no blood relation. At least Sapphire is still my cousin, I suppose that's something.

May 26th

The funeral was traumatic and sad. Sapphire and her brother Roddy managed to laugh though.

Everyone looked so glamorous, although of course it's hard to go wrong in black. I wore the black lacy skirt that I finally managed to get off Maria and a little black jacket that belonged to May.

Sapphire looked striking in my long black velvet coat, which she wore with a red rose in the buttonhole. She must have been a little hot, although she always claims that she has weak circulation. She and Roddy were consumed with hysterical church giggles at the moment when the vicar waved goodbye to the coffin as it slid into the incinerator or wherever it goes. Sapphire said it was a truly awful situation, hugely embarrassing, and her gut still aches from laughing. She is exhausted by the emotional trauma of wanting to stop and of trying to pretend to be crying. It was nerves and tension, she said, that set her off.

I sat between Dad and Stella. Stella had made
226

a real effort with her appearance and looked better than I have seen her looking for ages. She had her hair up and she wore a black, slim-thin wool suit with gold buttons. The professor looked rather sweet in an ill-fitting black jacket and small, thin black tie.

A gospel choir sang two very moving songs, one called 'Up where we belong'. The last stanza cheered me a little:

> Time goes by,
> No time to cry,
> Life's you and I
> Alive, today.

The professor read some Shakespeare. The last two lines were particularly stirring:

> But if the while I think on thee, dear friend,
> All losses are restored and sorrows end.

Later it was my turn to read and I stood a little shakily and made it to the front:

> Death is nothing at all. I have only slipped away into the next room. I am I and you are you: whatever we were to each other, that we are still. Call me by my old familiar name. Speak to me in the easy way which you always used. Put no difference into your tone; wear no forced air of solemnity or sorrow. Laugh as we always laughed at the little jokes we enjoyed together. Play, smile, think of me, pray for me. Let my name be ever the household word that it always was. Let it be spoken without an effort, without the ghost of a shadow on it. Life means all that it ever meant. It is the same as it ever was: there is absolutely unbroken continuity. I am but

227

waiting for you, for an interval, somewhere very near just around the corner. All is well.

Canon Scott Holland.

The penultimate sentence says it all. May waited for me somewhere very near and around the corner for the whole of my life. The passage is quite pertinent and makes me feel easier about the whole situation. I interpret it to mean that I must think of May in the same way now I know the truth about who she really is. When I got back to the pew, Stella whispered, 'It's been difficult, but we'll pull through won't we?' I nodded and smiled at her with my eyes.

June 5th

May has left me Waterstone House and a letter that I have read twenty times or more:

My dearest Anna,

I write this letter because I have not been myself for a while now and I can sense that it won't be long before my time is up. My limbs are stiff and creaky and life is very grey. Endless *ennui*. When I'm gone you will know the truth – you are my only child. Oh darling, I've wanted to tell you for so many years, but I haven't had the courage. What would you think of me? Would you have forgiven me? Do let us hope that God will be at mine end, and at my departing, because I am a weak sinner.

Once when you were about eight years old you came to stay with me for the weekend.

228

We went down to the stream and stood on the bridge and played Pooh-sticks. When we were walking home, you put your small hand in mine and said, 'Aunt May, I wish you were my Mummy.' That nearly broke my heart. Such a poignant moment. I never forgot it. I had to turn away from you that day and shed a few tears, but I managed to compose myself and I kissed you and said, 'Wouldn't that be lovely, darling?'

Of course I was weak and selfish not to hold on to you when you were born but the post-natal fear and depression swept through me, and I was treading in stagnant water. I couldn't see a way to bail myself out because it seemed so futile to even get out of bed and dress myself. For what? For whom? Of course I should have got dressed for you but I couldn't. I swear I couldn't. My condition was diagnosed by a series of doctors as a nervous breakdown. To me it felt like swimming against a strong current; I knew that if I tried to look after you we would both drown. It seemed impossible to care for you when the man I loved didn't or couldn't be with me. *The sun was very dim and the moon was very black.*

Please, darling, understand how difficult it was for me, in my mid forties, to experience such a profound disappointment in love. It really was my last chance to lead a normal life. I had yearned to settle down all through my thirties, to get married and have a child. No one believed that's what I wanted. Everyone thought I was a wildflower, rootless, nomadic, leading an adventurous life, writing books here and there and having passing affairs, but I was lonely. So lonely. You have no idea how long a Christmas week can be.

And then I met the only man I have ever really loved and he happened to be pinned in a torturous marriage which he couldn't escape from. In the first flushes of our romance he promised that he would leave her. He had sworn they hadn't slept together for five or six years. I believed him, but when I got pregnant and decided to have the baby, he wouldn't or couldn't desert her. She emotionally blackmailed him. She threatened to throw herself off the roof. She could hardly stand the sight of him but she didn't want anyone else to have him.

My friends said it would be difficult to bring up a child on my own and in those days it was much more frowned upon than it is today, although all that didn't matter to me. I didn't really care what other people thought.

You were so tiny and wrinkled and vulnerable. I just didn't think that I could cope on my own when I felt so emotionally volatile. It was the end of the affair and I was so distraught. Your father was a wonderful man, and I have left some of his letters and photographs for you in a deposit box. Mr Asquith has the key.

The situation has not been ideal for you, but please take a little comfort in knowing that I have always loved you as my own and I have prayed that you will understand and forgive me. I want you to have Waterstone and I hope it will bring you years of happiness. I would like you and Sapphire to share my few jewels.

And remember, darling, men are so much

more practical than women when it comes to affairs of the heart.

Forgive me, darling, for all this and more.

May.

It's a lovely letter and I understand what happened, but it is hard to forgive her for not confessing to me in person.

I'm here now at Waterstone, my house, Waterstone. I have written to Giancarlo to say he can keep the flat. Giancarlo and Head of a Cow can use it as their London shed. Maria is going back to Spain. She says she is going to train to become a weathergirl on television.

The professor wants to stay in the house, because he's teaching at Bath. He's going to rent a bedroom and bathroom upstairs and have the use of a small study downstairs. We will share the kitchen, dining room, conservatory, and everything else. It fits in quite well. I'm fond of the professor and I need the income.

Sapphire is coming to stay for the summer. She is as blown away as I am about May being my mother. She swears she never knew, although she thinks that May and I have similar eyes and cheekbones. Stella is very pleased that I know the truth. She says she had wanted to tell me herself years ago but May wouldn't hear of it.

Since the May-is-my-mother drama Nick and I have spoken every day on the telephone. He says he misses me. Sometimes he calls me very late and we chat for at least an hour, so perhaps he doesn't have other girls lurking under the sheets. Last night he asked me to join him for the weekend. My heart didn't bump like it usually does when someone I like asks me to do something exciting, but I was pleased to be asked. I want to take this one slowly. Perhaps I'll invite him here for a weekend at the end of the summer. It'll be the beginning of September, the shadows will be long on the lawn and we'll have blackberry tart for tea.